Message from the Author

A dusty manuscript hidden in the
deepest darkest corner of the
closet, can transform into a
great novel with a little
work and dedication.

C H A P T E R   1

▼

August the 12th 2005
11:22 AM

Darkness becomes light, death becomes life. I wanted to die, more then what is imaginable, but that would be something I would wait for. Death I feel is a prize I would have to earn. For so many men it is simply given to them, but not I.

As darkness slowly became light, it became clear that it was florescent, and I was being dragged through a hospital hall by men in white lab coats. My head spun with the comprehension of the day before. I would sooner forget then try to remember that. I had hoped it were just a dream, but no such luck would I have. Her face is all I see. The last thing I saw before the blackout.

The room they had taken me to I guess, was an emergency room. Judging by what I could see through blurred eyesight anyway. My head was migraine bound, and my vision was like looking through the bottom of a beer bottle after I had a few more then a few. There was a distinct aroma of rotting death all around like you would find in the morgue. Maybe I was dead after all, and this in-fact was not the ER. No such luck.

An odd looking man in a white lab coat sporting some thick bottle glasses entered the room. He held a briefcase in one hand and a clipboard under his left arm. An eager looking smile ear to ear covered his middle-aged face. He put the briefcase down and opened it. He pulled out a small flashlight shinning it in my eye. What a jerk I thought, I just woke up and this punk shines a goddamn flashlight in my eye.

"Tell me. What is your name?"

"John."

"John is it?"

"Yeah."

I guess that's all he wanted to know, cause he stopped paying attention to me and started to type away at a laptop he had sitting on his cross-legged lap. I rubbed my eyes at a futile attempt to rub the blur out of them, of course that didn't work. As hard as I tried I couldn't really focus on a damn thing. I thought for sure they must have drugged me up something out of this world.

"What am I doing here?" I asked.

"I'll ask the questions Mr. John. Thank you." He replied.

"Paddock. It's John Paddock." He said nothing in reply and continued to type away. I breathed deeply my own frustration. Without taking his eyes from the monitor he asked me.

"Tell me what happened?"

"Depends."

"On what?"

"On what you want to know."

"I want to know what happened on the island Mr. John. John Paddock."

"It's Paddock, it's just Mr. Paddock."

"Tell me what happened Mr. Paddock." He said with a hiss.

"It's actually Officer Paddock."

"Lets make this as brief as possible Mr. Officer. Whatever your name is." He said with a hint of hostility. I could tell this might take awhile.

"I'll try to tell you as much as I can remember on these drugs you got me on."

"Drugs? Who said you are on drugs?"

"Well I assume…"

"You assume? Assume what? That we drugged you with something?"

"Look I just figured I'm in a hospital right? So you must have injected me with something cause I cant see straight for shit." He paused for a moment.

"Rightfully so, but wrong. What you are feeling will soon dissipate Mr….uh John." He cleared his throat.

"Now from the beginning."

"It was yesterday morning…" He interrupted.

"Beginning with your name, please."

*   *   *   *

My name is John Paddock, Chicago special forces unit 001, and up until less then 24 hours ago I thought I knew it all…I was wrong. This is my story as I remember it, or at least what I can recall through all the trauma. I warn you now that what I am about to tell you may startle you…the truth is not always what you tell yourself what you want to hear, but in this case it's the only alternative. Darkness…I always thought it was a mere description of the opposite of light, a shadow created by a beacon in the night, but now I've come to find it has a much greater meaning.

It seemed like a day like any other hot day in the month of August, a day like any other in an average city, in an average persons life. All the norms going about there normal weekend routine, with their families, friends, significant others, whatever be the case. It was just your average everyday normal summertime Saturday in the city of Chicago. The beach packed elbow to elbow with sunbathers, as it would be on any other hot day like this, hot as in one hundred plus degrees. The sun baking bodies on the beach like an egg in a skillet, pale skin charred to a nice golden tan sunny side up and all. It was no speculation so many natives of the city and tourists could be found on the beach of Lake Michigan just off of Lake Shore Drive. After all this was the first hot summer weekend we have had this year. All those before were rained out and soggy. I myself have yet to enjoy the pleasures of the weekend. I had other duties to attend to.

But it was not just the beach alone that attracted the masses, not even close. There were of course numerous other activities that could be found in this great city. From our numerous museums, to our parks, and monuments. Or you could catch a ball game at one of our two great stadiums. Whatever you wanted to do, Chicago had much to offer, some of which I wished it did not.

There was a side to the city no person ever saw, I myself included. A dark side of decay that plagued the streets. A vial force hidden in the shadows and underbelly of the city. If the people knew of its existence, it would only drive them to a life of fear and hiding. There is a dark curtain that hides these vial men. Not a literal curtain that you can see and touch, but a metaphor for masked walking death and destruction. This is where my story of the dark curtain begins.

*   *   *   *

The Rogues

*   *   *   *

The downtown area skyscrapers looked as if they were nothing more then a blend of gray and silver, our chopper raced through them with unprecedented grace and agility. To the west a storm approached, it would arrive in the next couple of hours, still allowing for plenty of time on the beach for those that wished to wait. The chopper was black and a highly aero dynamic, well oiled machine of the 21st century. Very costly as well, about a quarter of one hundred million. A one of a kind that read Chicago P.D. across the sides in silver letters.

We had been on patrol since five AM, and my fatigue showed it to say the least. Yet another weekend on duty I thought. Nothing new to me really, I cannot remember the last time I took a vacation. Although I know it was more than two years ago. But that is the life of the commander of the prototype special ops team for this city. When I say prototype that is to say no one knows of our existence. As far as the general public is concerned, we are nothing more then typical cops. This is how it has been for the past two years. Our purpose? Quite simple, to pose a greater threat than a terrorist or civil uprising. To have the ability to control a situation without outside help from government organizations such as the F.B.I., Military, National Guard, etc. The Mayor wants a fully self contained city, in essence, his own little country.

The wind blew through the chopper making a howling sound like a wolf at the moon, singing it's somber song. My black bulletproof vest with its itchiness and sweat made for a very uncomfortable feeling. As much as I would try to fight it, in this weather it was impossible. Still I was no stranger to it. But I try none the less. The fingerless gloves I wore also presented an uncomfortable feeling. I could remove them and squeeze out half a gallon of sweat. My chin wore a two day old goatee. I have yet to decide whether or not I was going to keep it, a work in progress I guess you could say.

Across from me sat my partner Chucky. His cheeks full with chewing tobacco, a disgusting habit he hade made his trademark. He hummed an old James Brown tune, Motown being his favorite music genre. His love for old music was incredible, even though he was the same age as me in his mid thirties. He was a quiet shy man, still you never wanted to anger him, or he would show you the quiet ones are the one to watch out for. He was African American and very large, six feet seven inches tall, and about 350 pounds. Definitely, the largest one on my team. A good looking man with a shaved head. He liked to keep to himself but generally followed orders, most of the time.

Sitting to my left was Bobby, a young kid in his early twenties from New York. He was a rookie, to say the least. Bobby was the type that always managed to have an attitude problem, a real problem with authority, my authority. Even though he could be an asshole at times, He was definitely still one of mine. As far as his shooting capabilities go I would not trade him for anyone. He once shot down a chopper hosting a Cuban drug lord from five hundred feet away, with a simple nine. He was definitely the right one for the sniper position.

Mira…What can be said about the beautiful, talented, amazing Italian woman who sat next to Chucky. Mira was my fantasy as it were, but I could never seem to find it in me to tell her. She was my nonexistent dream girl. Someone I had to see to believe, in a sense like I was imagining her. She had a petite body small everything, from her rear to her breasts. A perfect body in my eyes, she was flawless. She had shoulder length brown hair. She was intelligent and talented, the best on my team, next to myself of course. She was however very by the book, which made for many unwanted confrontations. I was not by the book by any means. How could I follow a book that has not been written? After all we are just a prototype team. On duty she was very professional. But off duty on rare occasions, I had taken her and her 3 year old daughter out. She was very laid back and fun. But even now she sits upright. Her hands resting in her lap most proper.

Mira's husband, her daughter Ashley's father, left them when she was still pregnant. Ever since she has lost most, if not all faith in men. Only I have been able to slowly bring that faith back. Unfortunately, I am an asshole, or at least I play myself off to be one. That is why I don't think I am the one for her. But regardless I have strong feelings for her, and her daughter. If only I could express them better. My previous relationships have tainted me. Now going out to the strip club and getting a fine piece of tail, is my idea of a good relationship.

Jackie M-16. The oldest friend of mine. Long before our rogue team was formed. There was Jackie and myself. He sat in the far corner. Playing with his M-16 machine gun. He was dressed the same as us. Except for his "Have a nice day mother fucker" smiley face, T-shirt he wore under his vest. He was a character of sorts. We fought along side each other in Operation Desert Storm back in 1991. That is how we met. We were stationed just outside of Baghdad, and after the war ended we joined the force together.

Jackie had a love, no, an obsession with M-16's, it was his weapon of choice. He carried that gun with him wherever he went. Even off duty sometimes. Hence the name Jackie M-16. He was a good looking guy, kind of boyish. Though it never brought him much luck with women. They found him to be a little too screwed up in the head the majority of the time.

I sat there staring at Mira, lost in thought. I started seeing her off duty about six months ago. She said it was a bad idea to mix our professional relationship with a not so professional relationship. But after many nights of begging, and pleading she was mud in my hands, at least that's how I would describe it, mud. And still I have yet to kiss her. Sad really, no pathetic.

I could feel Bobby's eyes upon me. I ignored him, but it was not enough. His sarcasm would spew from his irritating mouth again.

"So Johnny, I see you eyeballing the merchandise over there, not bad eh?" Obviously he was referring to me looking at Mira, in which case he may or may not be right, but I figured I would play it off anyway.

"How do you know what I'm looking at Bobby? I think you assume I'm looking at Mira with impure thoughts in my head, when in actuality it is your own way of expressing your inhibited sexual desires, and your simply passing them or through me." He had no response.

"Besides assumption is the downfall of society. We as people assume what the other person is thinking based on our own thoughts alone. If we would just analyze the facts instead of constantly assuming the world would run much smoother." Bobby almost seemed unenlightened by my little B.S. statement.

"I only assumed..."

"Exactly. You assumed I was staring at Mira's body, but you were actually the one who was looking right?" He had no reply.

"Well?"

"Yeah your right I was."

"Actually I was just trying to get you to admit to it, and you did." I gave him a cocky smirk that I know he loathed. Bobby was only silent for a brief moment.

"So when was the last time you got any?" He had to ask.

"Oh. Your sister didn't tell you?" He gave me a curious, and concerned look. I continued with a chuckle in my voice. "She said the sex was so great. She asked me to marry her." I smiled with open arms. "Give me a hug brother."

For a moment there was dead silence, the silence was abruptly stopped after Chucky let out a loud wail of laughter, crossing his huge arms. Soon Jackie was chuckling in hysteria as well. Mira, on the other hand, was not so amused. She gave me a cold hard look of disappointment. It was a look I received often from her, especially when it came to Bobby. There were times I thought they had a fling going on behind my back. Mira assured me there was no such fling. I found it hard to believe but I accepted it.

After Chucky caught his breath and was looking rosy as ever. He added a little comment still giggling a bit.

"You should let me get some of that John." I looked at him and replied.

"Sloppy seconds eh Chuck?" he shrugged.

"Hey, I'm sure she's used to it." He let out a loud roar of laughter once more. His cheeks turning red as ever. I grinned with a nod to him. Laughter at Bobby's expense was a beautiful thing. Bobby looked furious as ever, grinding his teeth as he spoke.

"With all do respect sir. Making crude sexual references about my sister is a little inappropriate." I rolled my eyes.

"Inappropriate? You want to talk to me about inappropriate? Maybe I should teach you a lesson in discipline. Next time you think before you decide to ask me such a ridiculous question, you should know the answer is your sister after all." Chucky roared with laughter once more. Bobby's face turned red with anger. Still he suppressed it taking in a deep breath and calmed his tone.

"Your right sir. I apologize for my behavior, Sir." I folded my arms and leaned back, Mira still gave me that look, the look I hated so much. It put me to shame. Chucky spit out a huge black and brown wad of chew onto Bobby's Boots. Bobby looked at it with disgust.

"Lighten up kid. You got to be less uptight if you expect to last in this business." Jackie gave Chucky a nod of agreement.

"Hell's yes Chucky man." He said extending his fist to Chucky. They punched fists in a demonstration of strength hand shake. Jackie looked at all of us and spoke loudly over the whir of the chopper blades.

"Shit man, if I hadn't loosened up, I would still have visions from desert storm of Scud missiles flying up my poop shoot." Chucky replied to him still giggling a bit.

"Now that is something I would love to see." He again laughed a loud.

Bobby wiped the chew off his boot with a rag he had in his pocket. He cursed under his breath. Chucky watched him with a smile ear to ear. I could not help but chuckle a little. I tried to hide it as best as possible covering my mouth with my hand. Mira never took her eyes off me. Still giving me that look. I hated it so much. I felt like a child that disobeyed his mother every time I saw it. Sometimes I wish she would just tell me how she felt. Instead of giving me the cold shoulder.

I glanced around. It was time to take back order. "All right you sons of bitches! Lets get serious here! We all know today is the christening speech at Little Chicago. The Mayor, everybody and there mothers will be there. So we have to keep a heavy patrol over it, by orders of the Commissioner. I want your eyes peeled, your ears open, and your guns cocked!" I gave Bobby a sidelong glance awaiting a smart ass reply. But nothing, he was at full attention for once.

"Here's the current situation. The Mayor is going to make his speech in T-minus twenty minutes. That gives us a little amount of time to do a quick run of the perimeter." Bobby interrupted that of a school boy with his hand in the air.

"Hold up Captain. You already said all this shit in the briefing this morning. So…so why the hell you got to go and explain all this again?" My blank expression quickly turned to a frown.

"First of all, don't ever interrupt me again, and second you know the drill. We always do a quick debriefing before we go in." This time Bobby got the look of disappointment from Mira.

"He's right Bobby. Its standard procedure. You should know this by now." Bobby shook his head. "Look. All I'm saying is…never mind, fuck it, forget it." I looked at Mira as if to wait for the go ahead.

"Please continue John." she said in a soft voice. Now that she disciplined Bobby like a mother would a son it seems like.

"As you know, no one but the Mayor, and a few others know of our existence, and there will be a massive amount of civilians present. So the commissioner wants us to keep this on a low profile priority. The last thing we need is a damn reporter sticking his nose where it doesn't belong." Chucky pulled out a generous amount of chew and dropped it into his mouth. Full with chew and his gums flapping he said.

"If any reporters get in my way, they will have to deal with my sawed off up they ass." He smiled an ugly blackened teeth smile.

"Chucky I want you on the roof, Jack…" I paused remembering he prefers to be called M-16. He gave me a frown.

"M-16, I want you stealth, blend in with the crowd, pretend to be a common security guard." He interrupted.

"Oh, hell yeah, I get to play rent a cop today." Mira rolled her eyes in frustration. Just once I would like a serious briefing, I'm sure she thought the same as I.

"Bobby I want you as close as you can get to that big ass ship, and the mayor. Keep your eyes on him." I looked at Mira she was at full attention. The same as always.

"Mira, you will be with me. We will be patrolling the inner perimeter."

"Are there any questions?" I looked at Chuck he simply sat there and chewed. Mira's eyes moved from person to person. Jackie was rubbing his eyes. He had complained earlier about spending way to much time at the Titty bar last night. I looked at Bobby he wore an ear to ear grin.

"What is it?" He raised an eyebrow shrugging his shoulders looking at the floor.

"Well, when do we get some freaking action?" Action?

Is that all he cared about? I thought.

"Your reckless kid, and that type of mentality is going to get you killed. Now hopefully everything goes smooth today, and we won't have to see any action. At least that's what I want. I should expect no less from any of you. Understood?" A unanimous nodded reply came from all.

"Good. We should arrive shortly. Everyone got their weapons ready?" Weapons check, my favorite. Chucky raised his sawed off double barrel pump shot gun, he gave it a quick cock in acknowledgement.

"Check." Mira held up her Nine millimeter's in both hands crossing her arms like an ex.

"Check." Jackie looked at me with a grin.

"You don't have to ask me man. The name says it all."

He opened his eyes and mouth wide in excitement as he clutched his M-16. Finally was Bobby. He held the rubber handle of his knife with just his finger tips, and ran his thumb down the 12 inch blade. He gave a simple nod. I held up my chrome Desert Eagle 45 popping in a clip.

"Check."

✳   ✳   ✳   ✳

On August the 12th 1833,
Chicago became incorporated
with a population of 350.
August the 12th 2005,
Little Chicago Island
is born.

✳   ✳   ✳   ✳

Little Chicago. In the tradition of the highly successful tourist attraction Navy Pier. Little Chicago offers the finest in recreation. Built on a man made island off the shore line of Chicago. Three years in the making this island of steel and concrete was ready for its grand opening. What better way to celebrate the birth of a new island then with the birth of a new ship. The massive ship named the Windy Waters, its main purpose was to be used the same as a fairy. It would escort hundreds of people to and from the island. Little Chicago itself was made up of various attractions. Everything from a large shopping center to a grand hall, a large stadium, for what team was as of yet unknown. Even a church. It was truly an architectural site to see. We arrived at Little Chicago. Hovering above it in the chopper we could make out an enormous crowed has already gathered. "Let's circle around."

CHAPTER 2

▼

11:22 AM
The Windy Waters

*   *   *   *

"I remember taking the trolley…Oh my apologies. My name is Kenneth Gill, and this is my story."

*   *   *   *

I am a retired engineer, I worked for the Rockford corporation for a long time, thirty five years exactly.

Spending half my life there, only to retire with a less then adequate retirement plan. Leaving me no option but to work part time at a local drug store, an embarrassing position for a man of my talent. Still all of us must do what we can to survive. Even a young aspiring author I know by the name of Adam works there.

Much has been said about this new manmade island Little Chicago. I was excited to see what it was all about, so was my granddaughter Mary. She asked me the other day if we could go, I of course could not say no to those darling blue eyes, and of course my own curiosity invoked me as well.

We sat on the trolley, Mary played with her long golden hair, bobbing up and down on the seat in anxiousness. By her side was a pink book bag filled with hair ties, dolls, and the essential needs of a nine year old girl. Her face resembled that of her mother with blue eyes and freckles. I see a lot of her mother in her. They both have that curiosity trait that makes them ask me numerous questions about whatever pops up in there minds. Mary more curious than my daughter, being as young as she is everything is a mystery.

The ride on the old trolley was a bumpy one. The wooden interior creaked and cracked. It was the trolley that would take us to the Little Chicago docking area. Even though the ride was rough, whether it was from the old trolley, or the driver I could not tell. It was still better then taking a cab or a bus in this city, although, it resembled that of a bus, it was not a conventional trolley like those found in such cities as San Francisco, riding on wheels instead of track. And the city blocks came so frequently, the light always red. I could not help but sit there with anticipation, in hopes that this island is all it's cracked up to be. Constant news articles in the papers, all telling of its grand cathedral. Something I was looking forward to the most was just knowing they brought religion to the island was a surprise, what denomination I did not know.

We had just sped up from one light to the next, Mary jerked forward with a sudden stop, nearly falling out of her seat.

"Excuse me sir, but could you please slow down? You nearly threw my granddaughter from her seat." I said to the driver. He simply ignored me. "Sir please, I would appreciate if you could slow down some." Still there was no acknowledgement, he continued to drive like a maniac. Not even turning around or giving me a second glance in the rearview mirror. Mary looked up at me with a smile of anticipation.

"Are we almost there grandpa?" I placed my hand on her shoulder, and moved my head close to hers speaking with a low voice.

"As soon as this guy learns how to drive Mary." I spoke soft and low but still this time the driver heard me, He looked in the rearview mirror arching one brow. "Now you hear me." I exclaimed and again received no response.

Off in the distance I could see the grand island, It was gray as all the colors blended from this distance, and hard to make out one thing from another. We approached the docking area, traffic was indeed heavy in the circle, brake lights flashing rapid, horns blowing, the smell of carbon monoxide all around. Yes I was quite glad to have taken the trolley instead of my car.

Mary looked out the window at all the pedestrians and cars, without taking her attention away she asked.

"Grandpa. Why are all those people trying to take our idea?" I thought for a moment and laughed a bit.

"Well Mary, sometimes even when you thought you were the only person in the world who thought of an idea, to your surprise plenty more people thought of the same thing. Not to mention help from publicity." She turned to me and scratched her head.

"What's publicity?" Yes, attempting to explain the meaning of publicity to a young girl was not in my best interest.

"Never mind Mary." She looked at me with a frown of disappointment.

"Ask your mother when you get home." I continued, she turned her attention back to the crowd.

We sat there waiting for traffic to ease up, still the sound of horns and constant cursing of motorists continued. I looked at my watch, it was nearly time for the Mayor's christening speech. This would be the last time the ship would take passengers to the island until the speech was over.

I gazed at the grand ship, it put me in awe of its beauty. The perfectly shined gold trim, the etched Greek design, the white and black finish. I stopped and wondered how many tax dollars were put into the ship, not to mention the island itself, maybe donations were made from various companies throughout the city? I doubt it though, most likely it was donated to us by that weak country France as a means to kiss our behinds.

Suddenly a man in a red convertible pulled up along side of us. He was dressed in business attire, sporting a fine Armani suit and holding a cell phone to his ear. He seemed a little disgruntled with the man driving the van in front of him. His middle finger was used as a gesture to the man in front. I quickly placed my hands over Mary's eyes so she did not have to witness such behavior.

The man drove forward out of sight and I removed my hands from her eyes, she turned and looked at me.

"Grandpa, how come you covered my eyes when that man stuck his middle finger up?" I paused for a moment not knowing how to respond.

"Mommy says people who flip the bird are bad people, and they need to be punished." her words came as a surprise to me, to think my little granddaughter was knowledgeable of such profanity, and to think my daughter was teaching her that anyone who uses this gesture was a terrible person? I could not have this.

"Sweetie let me explain something. Sometimes grown ups tend to say and do things they don't really mean, just because a man does something bad, does not make him a bad person. He simply made an honest mistake, and I'm sure he regrets it and is sorry." She had a look of confusion on her face. I had spoken to soon as well, the man in the red convertible stood up in his seat screaming more profanity.

"Yeah fuck you!" He shouted as he swung his fist in the air. Mary looked up at me and said in a low voice.

"I don't think he's sorry grandpa." I shook my head in reply letting out a low breath.

A tall black man dressed in a black and white traffic guard uniform approached the driver. He walked up in a cool laid back manner, smile ear to ear and head cocked to the side.

"Its always good to see you were able to make another round in one piece, Joe." the guard looked around the bus.

"Bus looks intact too, impressive." he put one hand over his eyes like a visor looking behind the bus.

"No cops coming up behind you neither, that's good." He chuckled a little the driver did not seem as amused.

"Yeah good to see you too, Sam, you fucking son of a bitch." Sam extended his hand out to Joe for a hand shake.

"I'm just fucking with you man." He said with a smile as they shook hands, the vehicles in front of us had moved up a little but still we sat. Sam looked over his shoulder at heavy set balding man flailing his arms in the air in a white commercial van. The man laid on his horn, this only seemed to anger Sam.

"Hey! Who the fuck do you think you honking at ass hole!" Joe paused gesturing to the still huge amount of traffic in front of us.

"Can't you see their is still a shithouse full of mother fuckers in front of you?" Sam was using such foul language in front of everyone, and my poor Mary was being exposed to it all, though I doubt it fazed her, she was lost in another world looking out of her window at the amazing ship we were to board. The man in the van just flung his head back folding his arms in frustration.

Sam took in a deep breath it was only now approaching noon, but he seemed as if he had been working since five o'clock this morning.

"All right man. You better get these people to that ship, or you gonna have your self a shithouse full of pissed off mother fuckers." Sam wiped the sweat from his brow, the sun was hotter then ever with the coming of the midday.

"Man its going to be a hot one today." Sam backed away from the trolley onto a street median. Joe grinded the gears like it was his first day on the job, though I believed Mary enjoyed the little jerks, she cracked a smile every time she was thrown back in the seat. We pulled up along side the crowded curb, this was our stop. Mary was eager to get off the trolley and board the massive ship, I too was excited to see what wonders we would find on the ship. At first glance I was overwhelmed by the enormous crowed waiting to board the ship. People of all walks of life surrounded the dock.

"Grandpa I cant see the big boat." Mary was jumping up to catch a glimpse, I wrapped my arms around her waist and picked her up over my shoulder.

"Is that better sweetie?" I could not see her response but judging by her movement I could tell she nodded her head yes.

Far above us was a long brown plank with a silver and gold podium at the end extending from the ship, a little short man dressed in a Napoleon style outfit came walking out on the plank. The crowd was loud with mingling and laughter, not many noticed the man on the plank. His hands gripped both sides of the podium as he glanced around the crowd.

"Grandpa who is that man up there?" It was hard to tell even what his face looked like from here.

"Well, I'm not sure sweetie."

More of the crowd was silenced by the appearance of the man, many of the children looked in wonder as if it were amazing someone could be so high. A voice came from the speakers on the side of the ship.

"Attention! Attention! May I have your attention please?" the crowd quickly came to a hush.

"I'm sure you're all eager to get to the island, the mayor will be making his christening speech shortly, but before we go, there are some things I would like to discuss with you all." He continued on about safety precautions and how this would be the last trip the ship would make during the duration of the speech.

"So without further ado. If you could all use the stair case single file, we will be on our way. Thank you."

The top deck of the ship was laced with a well polished oak floor and finished oak seats.

"Grandpa I want to go downstairs." The extravagant deck was overwhelming with beauty, I could only imagine what the lower deck and dining area was like, though we would only be on the ship for a mere ten minutes for our short trip to the island, I still wanted to explore every aspect of it.

"Of course Mary, lets go see what fun we can have."

She gave me a little grin, I took her hand in mine and we made our way down a series of corridors each lined with gold trim and false candle light. At the end of the hall was the Dining area. It was filled table to table with passengers from previous trips enjoying there high priced meals. A man at a nearby table seemed to be eating some sort of sushi. It was a rather disgusting entrée, I never cared much for sushi. Anything that tastes and looks like it came out of someone's nostrils was not for me. Though I do enjoy the occasional eggs benedict which some might say looks as though it was extracted from someone's nostril. To the left of me was an older gentlemen and a young lady in a red dress sipping away at some fine looking red wine. The lady looking a little drunk. I was hoping it was his daughter seeing as she looked half his age, until I saw his hand grab her rear end. Must be another one of those retired hack Chicago radio jockeys still living off what little dignity he has left I thought.

"Grandpa can I go over there and look outside at the water?" I gave her a nod of permission, she scurried off to a nearby window.

A man dressed to impress in a long black trench coat and black fedora hat came walking up along side me.

"Pardon me buddy, but do you got a light?" I looked at him a little surprised at first, not realizing you could smoke on the ship, then I noticed you could smoke close to the bar.

"Well actually I don't smoke, but I think I may have a Zippo here." I padded down my pants pockets and my inner jacket pocket. The lighter was in my jacket where it has been for months, or at least since the last time I washed this jacket. It was gold and tarnished with an emblem of an eagle scooping up a field mouse.

"Here you are, It's my fathers old Zippo. He used it during the war. I take it with me wherever I go." The pasty faced man took the lighter in one hand that was covered by a black leather glove, his other was naked to reveal a sweaty palm holding the cigarette. He lit it and took in a deep breath, holding it in for a long time. I think it was his first cigarette in a few hours judging by the way he smoked it.

"Thanks pal I needed this." I decided to make small talk with my new mysterious looking friend.

"So what brings you to the island today?" he gave me a sidelong glance and gazed around the room as though he were looking for someone.

"Business." he simply said. Business? I thought. What could he mean? Maybe he was one of the mayor's men.

"I see well I'm here with my granddaughter for recreation. We came to see the Mayor's christening speech." he let out a small breathy chuckle filled with smoke.

"Yeah, the Mayor's speech should produce a big bang." he took in another drag with a diabolical grin.

"Really? Well what makes you say that?" He looked around the room never once looking me in the face with a bit of nervousness in his eye.

"Nothing…Nothing that should concern you. Just enjoy yourself." The man in the black trench coat gave me a smile and then with a nod he disappeared into the corridor.

CHAPTER 3

▼

11:22 AM
The Island duty

*   *   *   *

I was the newest addition to Little Chicago. It was my first day on the job, opening day and training day. Well I had already been training for this day for three months now. My name is Greg Armstrong. I am one of the first shift security guards for Little Chicago. Three months is what they told me. Three months till your job is to serve and protect the people of little Chicago. Three months till your first real day in the field. And especially three months till the big promised raise. Yeah I guess you could say I was more then a little excited about the whole thing. I mean after all I had seven kids to feed. I needed this job and this raise. I am a forty year old black man just tying to make it by.

The training was long and hard to say the least. My supervisor was always pushing me to the limits, trying to see if I had what it takes, yeah it was tough but I did it for my kids. I also did it for myself. It was time to stop bouncing from job to job, with no hope for a better tomorrow. Here, at least I had that hope. Today was definitely not a day I wanted to mess up.

I was making my rounds on the island, coming up to the grand outdoor food court and beer garden, a large area surrounded by a white picket fence with all sorts of trees and shrubs to enhance the whole island effect. Each tree was flown in by helicopter during the construction of the island, it took three months to fly in and strategically place all of them. Even though the whole thing is manmade, the island still has that appeal of something extraordinary, just the design and construction alone makes you think. Near one of the more popular fast food restaurants at least so far it seems to be more popular, anyway. There stood a tall Spanish looking man with long dark curly hair that came down over his shoulders from a black fedora he wore. He also was strangely dressed in a long black trench coat. Seeing as how it was hotter then Hades today, I thought it was a bit odd that someone would prance around in some freaking long ass trench coat. But who am I to judge how a man presents himself? Still I thought this mans unsettling glances around the area with those dark sunglasses on was a little suspicious. I removed my radio cell from my side.

"Hey Sam? Did, uh, the mayor arrive yet?" for a brief moment my heart skipped a beat when I saw what looked like a gun sized bulge in the mans jacket, I emphasize on the word jacket and not his pants.

"Negative Greg. He should be arriving shortly via the ship. Why is something wrong?" My first instinct was to sound the alarm, but I did not want to fuck things up today, so I refrained.

"Oh uh. Nothing, just wanted to make sure. Greg out."

I could feel my heart pounding in anticipation as I held my hand to my chest. What was I to do? Was this for real or was I simply imagining things? In all my training I never learned how to handle a panic situation. Me being the one to panic. All right calm down I told myself. Just assess the situation before jumping to conclusions. My finger ran slowly across the little black button on the radio. I could not take my eyes off the man in the black coat. Maybe he was just one of the mayor's men. He must be. Yeah that was it, just one of the mayor's men. I had come to assure myself that there was nothing to be alarmed about I was just jittery from today being my first day out. Suddenly, my assurances diminished. There was a shrieking scream from behind. My heart began to pound again like a roaring thunder. Sweat dripped from my brow. I was breathing so heavy I thought I might hyperventilate. I swung my head around. My hand was on my holster ready to draw my island issued taser. We were not allowed to use a conventional gun. Unfortunately, my supervisor said it had to do with insurance purposes, at least that's what he told me.

I ran into the crowed frantic and nervous. Afraid that my first day would be my last. Maybe I panic easy, but so what. At least this way things won't slip by me right? I pushed and shoved people to the side. I pushed an old lady she nearly fell to the ground, as bad as this may sound to you, I really didn't care. I had to protect these people in other ways. That was my sworn duty as an island officer. I heard another scream I looked to my surprise. It had only been one of the side shows going on outside. Weirdo's dressed in crazy clown outfits danced around the stage. The screams came from a mime no less, fucking ridicules. A mime for fucks sake. The mime looked at me and smiled, I smiled back flipping him off. His jaw dropped in shock. What an asshole I thought.

Turning back to the direction of the man in black I found him to be gone, nowhere in sight. The massive crowd only aided him. Maybe I dreamt the whole thing? But it seemed so real. Real as the hot sun that beat down on me. I'm just overreacting that's all. So much confusion I was confusing myself. Maybe I should go look for him and make sure everything is fine. As I was standing there minding my own damn business, this asshole comes running up to me.

"Greg! Hey Greg! Remember me?" A tall sunburned white man dressed in khaki shorts and a striped shirt stood in front of me.

"Nope. Can't say that I do." I took in a deep breath and wiped the sweat from my brow. The sun lurked over head like Gods barbeque cooking up human souls. The man looked at me through thick bottle glasses.

"Come on man. You can't tell me you don't remember the Juggler back in high school? We were the top dogs man." I tossed whatever he was talking about aside and looked over his shoulder for the man in the black trench coat. Only nameless faces could I see. The man whom referred to himself as the Juggler, put his head in front of mine to grab my attention.

"Come on man! The Juggler! You don't remember? We were the best juggling team in high school. Hey, are you all right man? You seem a little jumpy?" I understood what he said but could not comprehend the meaning. I was beginning to feel light headed. He spoke more but the words sounded like gibberish. My head started to ache with a splitting migraine. Everyone around me seemed to turn into dark shadows. No longer people of the living realm, but mere images of the spectral realm. Shrieks of madness surrounded me, no longer sounds of joy and happiness, now pain and echoes of sorrow. A nightmare was unfolding before my very eyes. I stood there motionless trapped in place, unable to move or even blink. I looked around at the shadows that surrounded me. They spun in circles around in perfect float with no legs. A small young boy covered in blood head to toe road a black bicycle with a skull on the front around me in circles. He wore an evil wide smile upon his face.

"You did it! You let them die! You did it! It's your fault!" the boy said with an eerie voice. He vanished into thin air. Another boy, the same as the last rode up around me on his bicycle. In a slow speaking low voice he started chanting.

"It's your fault. Your fault. Your fault. Your fault." he then vanished the same as the last. The world spun faster the shadows now becoming solid black.

A third boy rode up along side me. He stopped his bike and looked up to me with sadness in his eyes.

"Why did you let me die Greg? I was so young. You could have saved me." I screamed in horror and suddenly the world stopped spinning and everything was returning to normal. Shadows became human faces again. The sounds of sorrow faded into laughter. Everything was back the way it was.

The tall man from before stood in front of me. He placed his hand on my shoulder.

"Are you all right?" he asked with great concern in his eyes, and looked to the sky.

"I'm sorry I let them die. I'm sorry I did nothing. I was just a boy myself. Forgive me. I'm sorry. I'm sorry. I'm sorry." I blinked my eyes to see the tall man looking down on me through his thick glasses. He was dumbfounded, oblivious to what happened.

"What in God's name are you talking about?" I held my head in both hands. I must be crazy I thought. What the hell just happened?

"I'm fine. I just need some more meds or something.

Fuck that was intense." he looked at me puzzled as ever as he grabbed my shoulder to help me up.

"What was intense? Are you sure your okay?" I nodded my head. Of course I'm not okay. I just had the most fucked up vision I had ever had. Ever since I was 12 years old I have been on medication for chronic nightmares, but never before have I had a day mare. Especially one so real.

I remembered the man in the black trench coat.

"Yeah uh listen, it's just that its my first day on the job. You know its kind of getting to me, making me all nervous and shit. Say uh, You didn't happen to see a guy in a black trench coat around here? Did you?" He gave no response, he simply looked at me with a blank stare.

"I didn't think so." It was no use attempting to get a reply out of him, he seemed frozen in shock. Probably the first time anything like this has ever happened to him. Hell it's the first time for me, too.

"Listen man. You think you know me, I don't think you do. Right now I could care less if you do. So just fuck off, okay. Sorry if I'm being rude but I got more important things to worry about then juggling." His motionless expression turned to wide eyes of shock on his face. He seemed completely disoriented by the whole thing as he slowly turned around disappearing into the crowd.

I was still dizzy and needed to sit down. I sat on a stone bench just outside the main hall doors, resting my head in my hands. A young teen boy dressed in baggy clothes and a black baseball cap turned backwards sat there next to me. I clasped my hands together starring blankly at the brick walkway. No it was cobble stone. No, wait, it was definitely brick. A familiar aroma hit my nostrils. It was a smell I knew all to well. It brought me back to my high school days. Suddenly Jimmie

Hendrix was playing in my head. Even now in my darkest hour I could not indulge in the sweetness of it, the kind gentle relaxing feel. I was grown now and had responsibilities, not to mention random drug tests. Marijuana how I loved it so. A common drug amongst the masses. The most popular of all.

My first instinct was to expel the boy from the premises. On an ordinary day I would, but this was no ordinary day and I had more important things to attend to.

"Are you a cop?" he asked with a nervous slur. I gave the boy a sidelong glance.

"Are you an idiot?" I asked him as he took his cap off and scratched his head. There was a long pause before his reply.

"Uh…What do you mean?" he ran his hands across his knees back and forth.

"I mean, I know you been smoking pot. I fucking smell it fool. And your eyes are so goddamn red you look like a fucking vampire! Now to ask me a question that fucking stupid. I can only wonder about your mentality boy." he stared off into space mouth agape with out a single reply.

He cleared his throat and stuttered "So…are you going to arrest me?" It amazed me. This boy had no idea how to act in public on drugs.

"No. I'm not going to arrest you because I'm not a cop. And two I have more important things to worry about then a misdemeanor offence." He stumbled to his feet and disappeared into the crowed. I have had one hell of an interesting first day so far.

CHAPTER 4

▼

11:22 AM
The Dining Hall

✳   ✳   ✳   ✳

"Oh hello Mr. Johnson, Mrs. Johnson. I'm so glad you could join us today. Can I get you anything? Coffee? A drink perhaps?" A young attractive blond waitress holding a tray with coffee and glasses in one hand and a bottle of merlot in the other asked, as if she knew me outside of media attention.

"Oh uh, no thanks miss. My wife and I are fine thank you." the young lady gave a nodded reply with a quick smile before returning to the kitchen.

The dining hall was laced wall to wall with tinted windows that presented a privacy feeling for those inside who could still look out but no one could look in. It was one of the finer additions to the island. The walls themselves were formed into a half oval. Only the back wall where the kitchen and bathrooms were located was flat with no windows. An old fashioned mini bar designed that of the late 1930's early 1940's with an oak finish stood in the middle separated by half walls topped off with plant life. Only a few of the lonelier gentlemen planted themselves on the barstools with there leering eyes glancing around the room for a possible woman to use their lines on or to check out the lovely young waitresses walking about. Beautiful glass chandeliers hung over each table.

I had been invited by to the island by my good friend the Mayor. I insisted that I hated these kinds of social gatherings and refused to attend. Unfortunately, George had mastered the art of persuasion long ago. And I was soon convinced. Needless to say I still would rather be at home trimming the hedges or watching the grass grow then attending this bore fest. I was also nervous and full of anxiety. George was to make his christening speech today and all I could think about was that maybe this whole thing was a mistake.

Since that day, we have been friends. I remember that day like it were yesterday. It was a long time ago when George and I were very young. I remember it so vividly because I had begged my father to take me down to the beach even though he had business affairs to attend to. Eventually he caved. I had asked my father if I could walk down to the end of the pier. He told me it was fine as long as I did not get to close to the edge. He waited while I walked to the end. Below were some fish. All huddled together as if they had been awaiting my arrival. My natural boyhood instinct was to reach down and touch them. I laid down on my stomach reaching into the murky water of Lake Michigan. They all scattered in different directions. All except one. That one seemed to be just as curious about me as I was him. He seemed to stop in the middle and look up towards me with big bulging eyes. He was too far below the surface for me to reach. Slowly I stretched my arm deeper into the water. I nudged my body just slightly more over the edge of the pier. Still the fish was still. More and more I stretched till finally I touched his nose. He swam away swiftly. Now I was to far over the edge to regain my footing and soon I was falling into the waters.

I struggled for life. I could not swim and was drowning fast. With every last breath I cried for help. A young boy had been playing nearby and heard my cries. He quickly ran to the edge.

"Please help!" I cried. "Hang on. I'll be right back." he replied and ran down the pier. Soon there after my father came running. He outstretched his hand to mine hoisting me out of the water. That young boy who helped save my life was George, our future Mayor.

Over the years I have grown to become George's most trusted financial advisor. And his most trusted friend. With whom he reveals all his secrets. I begged and pleaded with him not to make this speech today. But to no avail. In his own words I am but a financial advisor. And this is a matter of national security, not balancing the budget. George has many friends but his enemies far out weigh his friends ten fold. I fear for his life.

My wife Ruth sat across from me. She wore a white lace dress I had purchased for her years ago. This would be only the second time she has bothered to wear it. Only on special occasions, like the mayor's presence does she chose to. Simply because George complemented on how lovely she looks in it. I told her the same thing the day she brought it home, but only from the mouth of another man could it be true. Her hair was white like the dress, she wore her hair up today. Another thing George has never hesitated to compliment her on was how much he loves to see her hair up. He claims it brings out the twinkle in her eye and she eats this up. However when I say such things I am laughed at and called a liar. I majored in business, not women.

"Henry? Did you remember to pack my pills dear?" She dug through her purse franticly her face buried in it. She placed a hand on mine across the table.

"Oh please tell me you remembered?" She said with despair in her voice. I rolled my eyes. This was an every day occurrence. Pills, pills, pills, that's all she ever talked about was her damned pills.

"Dear I asked you before we left do you have your pills? You said yes. So no I did not bother to pack them." She huffed flailing her arms in the sky cursing obscenities. I glanced around the room in hopes no one saw this display of embarrassment.

"You should know by now George that I always say I packed them and then end up not." Closing one eye, she pointed a finger at me.

"I'm beginning to think you do this to me on purpose." I folded my arms leaning back in the chair.

"Yes dear. My sole goal in life is to make you unhappy, which makes my life a living hell. Its exactly what I always wanted." she leaned back continuing to dig through her purse ignoring my mockery.

"Well doesn't it?" I raised an eyebrow.

"Doesn't it what?" she continued to dig without looking up.

"Doesn't it make your life a living hell?" I shrugged my shoulders. I had not an ounce of sense to what she was talking about.

"Yes whatever." I gave her a sidelong glance as she continued to dig. "Would you like me to see if I can get some acetaminophen?" She did not look up.

"Fuck it, I'll just have a drink instead." The doctors have diagnosed my wife with boarder line Turrets Syndrome. If she does not have her daily dose of meds she begins to shout obscenities and drinks heavily. Its really quite embarrassing.

"I really do not think now is the time to be drinking Ruth. You remember what the doctor said about your boarder line Turrets? Maybe we should just leave." With a frown she slapped her hand down on the table looking me right in the eye.

"Fuck him. And fuck you. Were not going home asshole. I'll be just fine you son of a bitch." I rubbed my face with one hand peering out through my fingers at the onlookers. They were talking under there breath about Ruth. It was easy to see.

A waiter was walking by dressed in a dark fedora, dark sunglasses, and a white apron wrapped around a black trench coat. Ruth held one hand up to summon him.

"Excuse me young man. Could we get some alcoholic beverages here?" The waiter ignored her with a quick glance as he returned to the kitchen.

"What a rude bastard! And what the fuck was he wearing anyway? It did not look like any fucking waiters attire that I ever seen." I rubbed the top of my nose with my thumb and index. I was truly now engulfed in embarrassment.

I knew I should have convinced George to cancel the speech today. I should have tried harder. Now I'm cursed to deal with my foulmouthed wife.

"You can't deny Henry that he was a rude mother fucker." I clawed at my face with irritation. I could not take much more of this embarrassment. I sat up brushing my blue and black suit jacket off.

"If you will excuse me Ruth I'm going to use the rest room." she interrupted.

"Well hurry the fuck up. George is going to make his speech soon." I rolled my eyes.

"Yes dear."

The bathroom was crowded with men in their best suits who worked for the Mayor. Every stall and every urinal was taken. The bathroom was just as fancy as the dining hall. marble tile and gold trim sinks. The stalls were all separated into little rooms with no visibility from the outside. The sinks were all adorned with there own separate vanity mirrors lined with round light bulbs. A single sink at the end was not occupied.

Two men dressed in black trench coats and dark sunglasses stood near the sink. I washed my hands to relieve tension that had mounted in them. I squeezed them together as the water ran down. The two men talked amongst themselves. I over heard one man.

"Yes, two men. They have been following us." he was speaking into a radio headset.

"Affirmative." One man noticed me looking through the mirror. I quickly averted my eyes back down to the running water. I noticed through the corner of my eye one man whisper to the other. They looked at me through the mirror. My heart beat faster and faster. I splashed water on my face. Hair had clogged the sink filling it with water. A single drop rolled off my chin like slow motion it hit the water causing a slow ripple. The only sound I heard was that of my beating heart. The bathroom emptied and only myself and the two men remained. One man stepped towards me. I stared at myself through the mirror. He reached into his jacket pulling out a 45. The gun was placed to the back of my head. I squeezed my eyes tightly together waiting for him to pull the trigger. I said nothing, did nothing. I was frozen in anticipation. I open my eyes, They were gone. I was alone.

Panting with relief, I nearly forgot to breathe. I had no idea what just happened. I must have been hallucinating. I steeped swiftly out of the bathroom. I passed the kitchen with a double-take as I peered through the glass windowed double doors. An empty kitchen was there. Curiosity consumed me. I had to know what was going on.

The kitchen was a mess. Aprons, chefs hats, and trays all littered the floor. Pots were left boiling on the stove and skillets were on fire. I grabbed an apron and doused the fire. What a shambles I thought. Where could all the staff be? I kicked an empty can of refried beans out of the way. A sticky note posted on the cabinet read. *"11:50 sharp. All Personnel return to the control room."* It was signed by a man named Wes Adams. That name struck a cord in my mind. I knew him somehow.

I scratched my head in confusion. There was not a single waiter, bus boy, or cook, to take care of the patrons. It would not be long before an angry mob of yuppies came bursting through that door armed with there wallets and credit cards demanding refunds. Or even worse, my drunken Turrets wife.

Maybe I imagined the two men in black trench coats. But I know I was not imaging this empty kitchen. I glanced around there was a pantry door ajar. Slowly I reached for the door handle, it cracked open to reveal not a pantry at all, but a long white plastered hallway that seemed to go on for miles. My heart raced again. My inner voice was telling me to turn around and pretend nothing ever happened, but my undying fear that something bad was going to happen to the Mayor today drove me forward.

The corridor walls were unpainted plaster. Numerous doors were all locked. The lighting was poor and dim and this only added to the zigzagging walls, making them concealed to whatever lied around the corner. I made my way through the endless zigzags, door after door was locked. The faint smell of carbon monoxide filled the air. A hollow sound grew louder and louder. A light began to beam from the end of the hallway. An iron fence door locked with a padlock was at the end off the hall. I peered through. It was an underground parking garage filled with motorcycles and gulf carts, the vehicles were probably used by staff to navigate the island.

Far off in the distance a man in an orange vest was talking to one of the men in a black trench coat from the bathroom. They were arguing about something inaudible. Suddenly the man in the black trench coat pulled a 45 from his coat aiming it point blank at the man in the orange vest forehead. He used the gun to point at a set of metal shuttered doors. They walked over to them. The man in the orange vest used a wall mounted keypad on the side typing a pass code to open the doors. A huge beam of light shined in from the outside, it was brighter then the morning sunrise, only it was midday. They were at the edge of the island looking out on the lake. The man in the orange vest stepped up to the edge with the water below. The other man put the gun away pulling out a machete from behind his back, concealed by the trench coat. In an instant my heart dropped. The man in black, swung the machete slicing it through the orange vest man's neck. His head separated from his body flying through the air spraying blood in all directions. His lifeless body fell neck first into the water.

I covered my mouth gagging on vomit. My stomach knotted. I held it shaking. A man was just beheaded before my eyes. Never have I seen such an inhumane sight. The sound of footsteps from behind grew louder and louder. I was in a state of panic. A witness to murder they would surely kill me next. I swung my head from side to side searching frantically for a way out. A door to the right of me read -**STORAGE**-. I prayed it was not locked. To my luck it was open. I turned the knob slowly not wishing to make a sound.

The other side revealed darkness. I fumbled around running my hand down the wall in search of a light switch. The room lit up revealing crates stacked high to the ceiling. One of the crates read in bold black letters. -**LIQUID EXLOSIVE CANISTERS**-. Another crate was filled to the brim with fine bottles of champagne. "What have you got yourself into Henry?" I whispered. The fine print on the crate with the liquid explosives read. -**Warning Contents Under Pressure**-. Use extreme caution. Do not drop. Explosives and champagne an interesting blend I thought, makes for an interesting dinner.

"Mr. Johnson." I turned swiftly to see the two men from before standing with there guns drawn at the doorway.

"We've been expecting you Mr. Johnson, but your late, how tardy of you to be so belated and deferred." All those words have the same meaning yet he used them as if not. He smiled smugly.

"How do you know my name? Who are you?" I stuttered as I spoke. The two men exchanged glances. One man had a small scar on his left cheek he spoke with a raspy voice.

"It does not matter who we are. Even if we told you no one would believe you." The other interrupted.

"Come on Mr. Johnson. Its time to go. Mr. Block awaits." Block? That name sounded all to familiar. It couldn't be, the one, the only Mr. Block? The one who was on trial for crimes against humanity and for conspiring to have some nameless politicians eliminated. He was also the former chief of police which put him at a higher position for leeway. The case was dropped but not until after the

Mayor had Mr. Block banned from ever returning to Chicago. As I thought about this one of them walked behind me and with one blow to the head from the handle of a 45 I was out like a light.

I came to, hand cuffed to a chair. My vision was still a blur but in a haze I could make out computers and desks but they moved in double vision. I blinked my eyes rapidly attempting to clear them up. In the corner my kidnapers stood talking amongst themselves. They remained unaware that I had regained consciousness, which is how I would prefer it to be at least until my disorientation faded. In the background I could faintly hear George had already begun his speech. I blinked a few times and my vision returned. But I wished it had not, for to my utter horror I saw a vision worse then the beheading. It was a man dressed in a white control room uniform hanging from the wall in a crucifix fashion. His hands and feet had been nailed to the wall. Blood ran down from the nails onto the wall in a slow trail. His neck broken leaving his head to rest on his own shoulder with a look of horror in his cold blue eyes. His shirt once white, was now stained red with blood. The shirt was so badly laced with bullet holes that it ripped straight down the center. Revealing a battered chest, most likely from a base ball bat, or possibly a crow bar. His skull was equally battered. Dried dark black and purple blood covered the one side of his half cocked head. This man had been tortured to death. And then strung up in a crucifix for all to bear eyes upon. These people were sick, and disturbing. What could they possibly want? Or maybe they were part of a malevolence sadistic religion.

More horror was to be found, another man lay dead next to me in his chair. Still griping a white greatest dad coffee mug in his right hand. This man however, had only a single bullet hole in his chest. Greatest dad I thought. How tragic his life be taken from his children like this. I myself bore no child. Ruth and I have been together for nearly thirty five years. And never did we consider the thought of having children. It was something Ruth and I just could not see happening.

The control room was small. Just large enough for four men. Four men and two dead bodies. A man entered the room rubbing his chin with one hand and gripping a semi automatic assault riffle with the other. The man was clean shaven about mid to late thirties. He looked at the man on the wall with a slight look of disgust. "Get him down." he exclaimed sternly "This is not a fucking freak show. Keep an eye on Mr. Johnson." He gave me a quick glance and returned his attention to the two men. "I will return shortly." My kidnapers nodded in agreement. "Yes Adams." I thought about the sticky note from the kitchen that must be the Wes Adams that signed it.

CHAPTER 5

▼

*   *   *   *

11:47 AM
Dark Clown

*   *   *   *

"Lets check it out John." Bobby said to me with that cocky attitude, I looked at him with a half grin. I was also a little excited. There was finally some action I thought, but of course I could not say that out loud. Or one of my team members might think differently of me. And of course, I could not have that. If they thought something excited me in my dull life it could screw up my whole relationship with my men and my woman. Mira had always been convinced that I was a man with no ability to enjoy myself. I suppose if I ever wanted to get with her I probably approached it the wrong way.

"Yeah John. He's right." Chucky said to me as he pulled the binoculars from his face.

"It definitely is a man on the breakers." Why was he hanging out on the breakers? Fuck if I knew. I took the binoculars from Chucky to get a better view.

"All right let me see those Chucky. I will be the one who says whether or not we go down." Focusing, I could make out what looked like a man in a long black trench coat that was flapping in the wind. The breakers were extremely rocky and dangerous. They kept the strong undertow from getting close to the island. A virtual wall of sharp jagged rock compiled in the lake. It was not uncommon for people to get caught hanging out on the breakers. Normally this would be the job of the lake patrol to take care of, but out of sheer boredom I decided why the fuck not.

Close to where the man was standing was a small fishing boat docked on the breakers. Why the fuck would you take an old piece of crap metal fishing boat on Lake Michigan? I thought. Lake Michigan was no joke when it comes to extreme choppy waves, that could easily take out a little tiny boat like that. As a matter of fact a storm was closing in from the west that would definitely capsize that little boat. This man had to be on drugs I thought. What other explanation could there be. A little Dust, maybe some Acid.

"All right take us in closer." I said. The driver dove down quickly and smoothly with great grace.

"Hey nice job, Porky." I was not really sure what his name was. He was new. Our last flier had been terminated after he was caught pocketing Eight-balls of Cocaine that we compensated from a Cuban drug lord. Rumor has it, he cut the Blow right on the commissioners desk.

We hovered above the man on the breakers just enough to keep him from being blown away by the whir of the chopper blades.

"I don't know exactly what the deal is with this mother fucker, but I will bet any of you he's fucked up on drugs." Mira gave me a quick nod of agreement. Bobby on the other hand had to put in his two fucking cents.

"Cool Johnnie boy. Let me fuck with him. And I'll show you the right way to handle this situation" I could not take it anymore. I had to do it. The urge could no longer be controlled. I knew this was not going to look professional. But fuck it. I gave Bobby a swift crack to the jaw with the back of my fist flinging his head to the side. I said nothing and in return he simply rubbed his jaw staring at the floor. Mira gave me that look. And once again I found myself downing my head. My cheeks were rose red with embarrassment. Why do I always let her get to me? I thought.

I picked up the horn. "You there. On the breakers. State your business." The man continued to dig into the rock with his bare hands. I had no idea what he was doing. His coat flapped so hard in the wind he looked like a super hero with a cape.

"Sir, I'm afraid I have to ask you to return to your boat and vacate the breakers. The storm is coming in and it is to dangerous for you to be out here." I was blatantly ignored by this man as he continued to do what ever it was he was doing. M-16 picked up his gun and aimed it down at the man looking through his sniper scope.

"You want I should take this guy out John?" I moved his gun down with my hand shaking my head.

"There's no need for that M-16." Bobby was feeling his jaw as if I broke it. Chucky just put his head back and chewed his tobacco. I was losing interest from my men.

"I said get off the fucking breakers now!" I had every ones attention, including the man below who looked up over his shoulder at the chopper hovering above him. Then he quickly returned his attention to the rocks and then turned around back to his boat. Bobby muttered something under his breath. I grabbed him by his bullet proof vest he cringed in fear that I would strike him again.

"What did you just say?" I demanded. He closed his eyes turning his head to the side, to avoid a possible strike.

"I simply said that went well, Sir." He said, as if there were no sarcasm to that.

"You shut the fuck up Bobby. I am sick of your bull shit. Or maybe I should give you a lesson in hand to hand." I could see in his eyes the sarcasm building up. He had something to say and he would have said it.

"I would kick your ass, Sir." Just as I was about to lose it Mia peaked her head between us.

"That's enough." We kept our eyes locked on each other as we slowly pulled are heads away.

"Both of you are acting like children, and as your commanding intelligence officer I have to say this is unacceptable behavior."

I wiped the sweat from my two day old goatee. "I don't believe this shit. Here we are the most elite law enforcement team in all of the city, and were fucking telling some asshole to get off the breakers." No one replied but I could see in there eyes total agreement even from Bobby.

"Alright, lets circle the Island a few times." With that I looked at my watch, the face read 11:59 AM, the mayor was about to start his speech.

Chucky dropped some chew in his mouth and hummed an old sole tune. Once again I found myself eyeballing Mira. Unprofessional glances up and down her sleek figure. She had her head turned out watching the area below. Which is what I should have been doing as well, but of course I could not draw my attention from her. Even with a bulletproof vest on, her perky breasts could be seen heaving up and down with every breath she took. But it was not just physical attraction that drew me to her. Not in the least. Just the other night I had taken Mira and her daughter out for pizza. She always found ways to make me happy. Unfortunately, sometimes I was unsure if it was just me she was trying to make happy. It always seemed that whenever we were alone away from the team, especially Bobby, we always got along. It was something I wished would happen whenever the rest of the world could see.

I was completely lost in Mira's beautiful hair When Jackie rudely interrupted. He always picked the worse time to do so. I was in total ecstasy and then M-16 has to ruin it for me.

"I don't understand it man. Its like the street cops got the city on lockdown or something. Like they got all the scum's under their control. Know what I mean John?" Jackie always asked the most obscure totally out of the blue questions. Sometimes I wondered if a scud missile really did fly up his asshole and went straight to his brain.

"Yeah Jack. I know what you mean." I could feel a long conversation of rambling coming on so I folded my arms across my bulletproof vest and leaned back. Jackie was a good friend of mine and long time partner but his grasp on reality was weak to say the least.

"I've been thinking about it man. And lately everything in the city has been real quiet. Like the scum's been paying off the cops. Course that don't effect us, cause were top secret special forces and shit right? We don't do that street patrol shit. Know what I'm saying?" I nodded my head as if I understood what the fuck he was talking about.

"But maybe the scum's got to the street cops some how. Or maybe there is something else going down in the city." Chuck spit his chew on the ground. I looked at him and frowned.

"Come on man. don't be spitting that nasty ass shit all over the place." he let out a loud chuckle as he proceeded to put a whole big hand full of chew down his mouth.

Jackie continued I rolled my eyes. "Just the other day I seen this dude, dressed up in this fucking trench coat outfit deal. Talking to a cop. It didn't look to legit know what I'm saying?" I gave him a side long glance.

"You mean like that mother fucker down on the breakers?" He nodded with a point of his finger down below.

"Yeah just like that fucking guy." Mira shocked and surprised everyone when she suddenly joined the conversation something she seldom, if ever did.

"Yes. I have been seeing a lot of men dressed like that around the city, lately." Mira looked around from one of us to another we were all in awe of her comment. Not that it was anything spectacular. Just the fact that she spoke.

"Well what are you all looking at?" all of our heads turned the other way.

"I can join the conversation once and a while cant I?" she asked us all. Chucky looked at her and started talking with his mouth full smacking his gums.

"Its just that you never talk Mira. Nothing personal girl." She shrugged glancing from one of us to the other. We all shrugged and nodded in agreement.

"As I was saying. I saw this man in a black trench coat and sunglasses, with a black hat on. Talking to a swat team." I rubbed the center of my nose between my eyes.

"Look its probably nothing. Some fucking government officials or something." Chucky spit out more chew. I rolled my eyes with irritation. He looked at all of us uncrossing his arms and leaning forward.

"Most likely some assholes working for the Mayor. Just another excuse to waste tax dollars." Bobby's silence that I had been enjoying so much, had to come to an end.

"Yeah kind of like us. Eh Johnny boy? Another waist of money." He nudged my arm with his shoulder before I could do a thing. Mira cleared her throat changing the subject.

"What time is it John?" I looked at my digital police issued watch on my wrist.

"Damn! The mayor is going to start his speech soon."

We all looked out down below from the chopper simultaneously, but instead of noticing the huge crowd of people gathered around the mayor. I noticed a funny dressed clown looking man jumping onto a yellow speed boat that had been docked at the island. The clown threw the captain off the side of the boat into the water, and took off with the boat. He was speeding away towards the breakers.

"All right we got action here. Follow that boat and take us in close." The boat was fast, one of those fast tour boats that was also used at Navy pier. But the chopper was faster, we soon got close behind him. Hovering low to the water the waves were so choppy that they were splashing up inside the chopper. He left a huge wake behind him that caused a ripple effect to other boats in the area.

"Stop the boat now! This is Chicago PD!" Bozo turned around and flipped me off.

"That's it! Your ass is in serious jeopardy now asshole!" Bobby leaned over, sniper riffle ready.

"You want me to take his Cookie the clown asshole out boss?" I shook my head.

"No. Take us down on top of him. I'm going to jump on the deck." I said. The boat jumped a wave. The clown nearly lost control swerving to the right and left.

"Are you sure that's the smartest Idea John?" Jackie asked.

"No. Not really. It may be the fastest though." I said. Even though the boat had a large area designated to passengers, jumping on it still seemed like a bad idea at this speed. We were no more then five feet above the boat. The clown never turned around to notice me.

"Alright, here it goes. I'm going to try and stop the boat. Porky! Maintain position, keep her steady I'll let you know when I'm ready, Then I want the rest of you to join me." I glanced around, everyone was in agreement with simultaneous nods. Chucky, who was nearest to me, grabbed my hand holding it up, are forearms made a V-like shape.

"Be careful man." He simply said. I said nothing in return, simply swallowing looking down I prepared myself, and with that I took a deep breath and was airborne.

The wind was so strong that it felt as if my flesh was being ripped from my skeleton. Tear drops shot from my eyes from the force of the wind. The landing did not go as well as I hoped falling on my left knee, making a loud thud when I hit the boat floor. I was in pain but had to react fast. I rose to my feet drawing my 45. My heart raced and I was unsure if this clown was even armed. Hand in hand, I aimed straight for the back of his red dread locked head.

"Like I said before. Stop the fucking boat now, and put your hands in the air!"

$$* \qquad * \qquad * \qquad *$$

Castration for the soul

$$* \qquad * \qquad * \qquad *$$

The boat was now anchored, and the rest of my men had joined me. Guns all drawn though the clown had no weapons on him. We were out there past the breakers the city sky line looked as if it were all drawn together, in shades of gray black, and white, and one blotch of red from the red building. The boat rocked back and forth, up and down from the large choppy waves of Lake Michigan.

Our perpetrator the Clown, was not your typical looking clown. More of an evil clown dressed in black and red clothes with black and white greasepaint. He was painted up with an evil look on his face. He reminded me of this great underground rap group I know from Detroit.

"Alright. Mind telling me who you are? And don't tell me your name is Violent J, or Shaggy 2 Dope. Cause you don't look like any *Juggalo* I've ever seen." He laughed out loud throwing his head back.

"I'm fucking Krusty the clown pig!" His sarcasm reminded me of Bobby. I decided to do what I would to him swiftly kicking the clown in his shin. He grunted grabbing his shin.

"Listen Bozo. Your ass is lucky I did not let my man here blow your fucking head off. Trust me, he is willing and able. So I suggest you start talking." Mira looked at me.

"Maybe we should just cuff him, and take him back to the station." She suggested. I stared the clown up and down. He reminded me of a time.

"No. Something's not right." The clown winced in pain. Mira looked back and forth to the clown and I.

"What? What is it John?" I scratched my head. The clown was so familiar to me, as if I had met him somehow before. Of course, it hit me, he was one of those show clowns from Navy Pier. I remember when I took Mira and her daughter one day to the Pier and we watched one of his shows.

"That's it. Remember that time when we went to Navy pier and saw that clown show?" She nodded.

"Well this is the guy. This is the guy that took your daughter up on stage for one of his acts." The clowns eyes moved rapidly back and forth from Mira and mine.

"I never seen you two before. I don't know what your talking about." Why did this show clown suddenly decided to steel a boat I wondered. I whispered into Mira's ear so he would not hear.

"What do you think? Ulterior motive?" I said

"Its possible." She said.

"I just find it a little odd that this guy is stealing a speed boat today, of all days, on the fucking opening day of the Island."

"I agree John. Something's not right."

"I mean am I wrong Mira? I'm right, right?"

"No. I agree John."

"Good. I'm glad we could come to an agreement. It's always a good idea to agree with your commanding officer Mira."

"Agreed." She said.

I looked at the clown, he rubbed his eyes.

"Alright asshole, what is your motive here? And don't tell me you liked the boat so much you decided you were going to drive it all the way to Michigan." He simply replied with a big wad of spit that came out of his mouth and landed on my pants. It did not help his situation any more then what he said next.

"Fuck you pig! I liked the boat so I stole it." I put my gun straight between his eyes resting the tip of the barrel on his skin, and with a low voice I said.

"You better fucking give me some straight answers clown boy. Or I swear to God I'll splatter your crazy clown ass brains all over this boat." Mira grabbed my arm.

"Let me handle this one John." I gave her a nod and stepped back. Just when I thought she was going to do things by the book, she shocked me. Her gun was aimed dead center at the clowns penis. She had this look in her eye like do not mess with me prick.

"Listen up! You will do exactly as my partner says. You will answer all his questions, and you will cooperate, and if you don't then I will put a bullet straight through your dick hole, and watch the bullet fly out of your ass." All heads were lowered with amazement. All except, the clown who looked as though he was going to piss his pants. I had a small grin on my face as I rubbed my temple with my head half cocked to the side.

"Nice job Mira. I totally agree." I moved close to her and whispered in her ear. "Hell I didn't even know you had it in you." She composed herself, brushing dirt off her vest.

"Yes. Well, sometimes you got to hit these guys where it hurts." Chucky and I exchanged glances, he crossed his legs with a wince. The chopper hovered about twenty feet above us, causing a ripple in the water. I reached in my shirt pocket for my bottle of Tylenol.

"So why did you take the boat?" I asked as I popped four or five pills. He looked at me then back at Mira.

"I took it cause...I don't know." I threw my hands up.

"What kind of a fucking answer is that?" He was staring at Mira.

"Don't look at her, look at me, and give me a fucking real answer. Or maybe I will let her to do to you what she said she would." He turned his head to me shaking mine quickly.

"Ok then. How about that answer." The clown swallowed. Sweat dripped off his face washing away a little of his greasepaint. The tension mounted in his eyes.

"I was distracting you." He said with a low tone. Mira and I exchanged glances. What was he talking about? I knew there was a lot more to all this.

"Distracting us from what?" He rubbed some sweat from his cheek, exposing his pale skin.

"I was supposed to get you to arrest me, and take me back to the station. So that you would be away from the island." My heart was beating fast. I looked back towards the island.

"Why? What is going on at the island?" He shook his head, grinning slightly, with a look of mischief.

"You stupid fucking pig. This is none of your concern. This is way bigger then you, or your useless excuse for a team. We walk the shadows, and the night, you never even saw us coming. You'll never even know we we're there."

I frowned "What the fuck are you talking about?" his endless chatter about walking the night caused me to lose my grip. In an instant, my fist met his jaw, flinging his head off to the side as blood flew out. The clown spit a load of blood from his broken jaw. With one eye shut, and the other focused like a hawk on me, he looked like that of a demon spawn, ready to strike. No cuffs held his hands, only the barrel of a gun kept him at bay.

"Everyone's going to die." His words and voice were sincere, as if he had no doubt in his mind of this. One side told me this was a mind game and nothing more, and the other felt a little distraught.

"Stop fucking with me clown boy." His look of evil had grown steadily worse then before.

"Who's fucking with you pig? I just speak the truth." I wiped the sweat from my brow. It was close to one hundred degrees out now. And my armored suit was like an oven.

"I'm giving you till the count of three to tell me the truth. The real truth!" I gripped my gun tightly, so tight my knuckles ran white.

"One." He shook his head slowly, with one brow arched.

"I already told you pig...your all going to die." I was enraged with anger. Never before had I felt this much hatred for a suspect. I had know idea why. Maybe it was the fact that he had his filthy hands on Mira's daughter just last week. I could feel the trigger with my index. It was pressing into it, ready to pull.

"Two." The clown rolled his eyes.

"What? What do you want from me pig? Huh? You want me to just fucking tell you everything. I don't think so, or I will be just as dead as you." My patience wore thin. Why was I wasting my time with him. Lives could be at stake. I had no more time for bullshit.

"Three." The clown simply looked at me and smiled, which turned into a haunting laugh. Who was this guy? Was he insane? My head spun. I received no answer. I was furious with anger. Then suddenly I lost it. For that brief split second I can recall pulling the trigger and closing my eyes. When I opened them, the look on the clowns face was so pain revealing it was frightening. I glanced down to notice a pool of blood filling in his lap around his crotch. I had done it. I did exactly what Mira said she would do if the clown did not cooperate. Except instead of her pulling the trigger, it was me.

Chuck's mouth was wide open the chew inside fell out like a big black chunk of mud from his cheek. His eyes were just as wide. Even Bobby just stared at the clown in a daze. I was speechless too. This was not standard procedure, not by any means, this was a nightmare. Now I could face trial, and being stripped of my badge. Get a hold of your self Paddock. This was not the time. I had to get back to the island. The mayor's speech was already in progress.

CHAPTER 6

▼

*   *   *   *

12:15 PM
The Christening

*   *   *   *

The crowd was huge, the sound of thousands of voices echoed through my ears. We were to far back to hear exactly what the mayor was saying, there were just to many people around. Had we arrived sooner we may have been close enough to see and hear, but at my age this was just pointless to me. Mary on the other hand wanted to watch the mayor's speech. Though even if she could hear him, she wouldn't understand what he was talking about. She was far to young for a speech like this. Mary sat perched atop my shoulders, her weight and my back just did not seem to agree.

"You know Mary. If you get much bigger you will be carrying me around." She looked down at me with a smile.

"You so silly grandpa." She replied with that cutesy voice. Just above us, a police helicopter flew in, it hovered just above the Grand Dining hall.

"Look Mary. A helicopter." Men dressed in bulletproof vests, and geared up heavy with weapons and ammo, emerged from the helicopter.

"I wonder what there doing Mary?" She looked at the chopper and then the mayor, and back to the chopper.

"Maybe they are just part of the show." She said confidently. I thought about it for a moment, it was possible but not probable. Still I had no wish to worry her.

"Yes your probably right." After the men descended from the chopper onto the roof, the chopper took off in the direction of the hospital. Its not everyday that police are launched in by helicopter onto a tourist attraction, especially ones that are dropped down atop the dining hall.

The heat had risen to more then one hundred degrees, and this gray flannel sport jacket I was wearing was not comfortable in this heat. From watching the weather last night I should have known better. The arm pits of my jacket had darkened from sweat. Only a fool would still be wearing this thing, unfortunately I was that fool. It's my favorite flannel after all, so I couldn't leave it behind.

I gazed off to the west, storm clouds were on the horizon. Even though I had no desire to experience a storm, right now seemed like a fitting time to cool off. Even Mary dropped little droplets of sweat down on my shoulders, and she wore just a simple little yellow sundress. A large sweaty man, wearing a tank top that revealed his hair covered back, stood in front of us. It was a disgusting, and a repulsive sight to see, I tried not to step to close, but the crowd pushed me forward.

I attempted to ignore the man in front of us and notice the beautiful lake that surrounded. The edge of the island was lined with black steel fencing that formed the shape of a wave. A stone bench lay every ten feet or so with two stone planters on either side. All of the benches were currently occupied by onlookers of the mayors speech. In the two corners at the edge were two huge square stone planters with Greek art etched into the sides. Tall oak trees blossomed from inside these massive planters which you could not see the top of. For something man-made this was a beautiful island.

*   *   *   *

*The name Chicago comes
from the Indian word
Meaning "Great," as in,
great city.*

*   *   *   *

Suddenly, the Mayor's voice could be heard with crystal clarity. It sounded like he was standing right behind us. That's when I tuned to notice the huge speaker above us mounted on a light post.

"Grandpa I can hear him now." Mary said with excitement. I looked up to her with just my eyes seeing only the bottom of her chin.

"Yes, dear. Lets hear what he has to say."

"Well now, I guess we have audibility in the back there. Great. We were experiencing some technical difficulties. You know how new things are, got to work out all the bugs. But that's great that are crack team of electricians here could fix the problem in time. Thanks guys. Back to the matters at hand, after the christening, there are a few more important announcements I would like to make to you all. I stress the fact that they are extremely important, not just to you as a whole, but to all of the city, as well."

The mayor sounded nervous, his words came out fractured. I wondered about his big important announcement, about the heavy patrol in the area. I suddenly felt uneasy, I needed to sit down.

"I'm sorry Mary, but I'm going to have to put you down sweetheart." I gently lowered her. Feeling dizzy, I stumbled to a stone bench that was not occupied. As I fell down onto the bench. A security guard with the name Gregory on his name tag came running by. He stopped briefly to ask if I was alright, when I replied that I was fine, he ran off in to the crowd without a word.

✳   ✳   ✳   ✳

The Black Out

✳   ✳   ✳   ✳

After I stopped to ask the old man with his granddaughter if he needed some help, I continued to run, on and on. Never even knowing were I was going, or what I was doing. Was I tripping out? Or was this a dream? Or is it drugs? The man in the black coat, who the fuck was he? Why do I care so much? My first day on the job and I already was experiencing panic attacks, that's when it happened.

The whole world was in black and white, with streaks of blue and gray blurs. Red flashes like lightning filled the sky. The world moved slowly. I could feel heavy wind at my back but the leafs on the trees remained motionless. It was like a painted picture, all was still. I looked down at my arms and hands. They were so small, like a child's hands, Was I a child again? Looking around, everything was different. The island and the people were gone. There was nothing left but a vast rusted old playground, in a park by my house. It was where I grew up on the south side, but that was more then thirty years ago. That park no longer exists. They bulldozed it to build high rise apartments there.

I remember playing in this park long ago, on Sunday afternoons, after church my mother would take me and my brother when we were young. My brother was to young to play on his own, and I was too irresponsible to watch after him at the time. So my mother would simply take us together. We did not have a lot of money, but my she always found ways to keep my brother and I entertained, none the less.

I began to walk through the old condemned park. The grass had grown so high without maintenance that it flopped over on its side moving slight with the breeze. The trees in the background were still, not moving with the wind like a portrait, only the foreground moved.

I still remember the day they closed this old park. I was there, watching from my bedroom window, it was the day my nightmares began. There I sat with a broken leg wanting nothing more then to play outside. There were about six kids playing around the swings and slides. They laughed and played, but for some reason, as hard as I tried, I could not recall their parents to be anywhere in sight. Another kid walked up to them out of nowhere. This kid went psycho, he had a gun and started blowing other kids away. He shot and killed all six kids. He was young, no more then my age at the time. They locked him up in a mental hospital. That's were he lives even to this day, or so I have heard. It wasn't long after, that they condemned this park. Closing it down forever. They said the pain was etched to deep into the parents and residents minds to leave it the way it was, it was especially etched in my own mind.

I remember walking past the park one day shortly after they shut it down and a group of young hoodlums came up to me.

They simply asked, "Hey kid. Want to get high?" This was a mere three days after the whole park massacre and I was having several nightmares. I was frightened and ran the other way as fast as I could with a cast and crutches, I ran through a hole in the fence into the playground, I tripped on a piece of wood falling and breaking my other leg. I laid there helpless and screaming in pain. The three hoodlums towered over me as I lay there. They looked down at me and pointed. They laughed loudly at my misery.

"Stupid kid. Your that little bastard that just sat there and watched. You probably got off on it, sick bastard. You let all those little kids die in the park!" They took turns spitting on me, and laughing. After they had their fun, they left me there to die.

From that day on, I started to experience panic attacks, and my nightmares grew steadily worse. I had to receive constant medical treatment that was far to primitive at the time to do me much good. My mother fell deeper and deeper in debt. I still blame myself to this day for putting her in an early grave. She passed on when I was just fifteen, leaving me to take care of my little brother. It took nearly ten years of therapy for them to get me back to normal. Up until now I have been fine.

As I made my way through the park, I felt an eerie chill down my spine. I heard a squeak from a rusty chain. I turned around. Two empty swings swung in unison and suddenly froze in midair, turning into a portrait. I walked backwards, not taking my eyes from the swinging ghost like sight. Voices of young children howled through the air in dark eerie chants. I tripped over something and fell on my back. When I got back on my feet, I nearly fainted again. The dead body of a small boy lay facedown in a pool of blood in the sand box. Out of the shadows a voice called out to me.

"Stupid kid. You let those little kids die!" It was the voice of that hoodlum from so many years ago. What in God's name was going on? Why was I here? From around a tree the three hoodlums appeared. They were different now. They were dressed in black trench coats, and dark sunglasses, with black fedoras. I stood there motionless. I could neither run, nor scream. I was paralyzed. It was surreal. They moved in slow motion with grins bigger then what could conceivably fit their faces.

"I didn't let anyone die." I muttered in a low tone hardly audible.

"We saw you do it kid. You were there. You could have called for help or told someone." His voice slowly changed that of something demonic. I shook my head as the three hoodlums in black trench coats approached me closer.

"I swear there was nothing I could do. It was too late." Suddenly one of the hoodlums in the middle grabbed me by the neck lifting me in the air.

"Your right kid. It is too late." He lifted his sunglasses revealing empty eye sockets.

I opened my eyes, I was back on the island laying on a stone bench. Raising myself up with one hand, I rubbed my eyes with the other. I looked around, the mayor was still making his speech. I noticed one of those suspicious looking men in black talking to a police officer.

*   *   *   *

The Deceitful One

*   *   *

Everyone was in position. Mira was patrolling the inner perimeter while I took the exterior. Chuck was on the roof. Jackie was checking things out incognito, dressed like a security guard. And Bobby was positioned on the ship about to be christened. I stood atop marble steps that lead up into the main shopping center. The steps descended outward down as they went. From this vantage point I could see the majority of the island, and had a unquestionably clear view of the ship.

I found myself taking a quick trip down memory lane as a man named Wes Adams ascended the stairs. Before I became leader of the special forces, I was partners with Wes Adams. A smile ear to ear over took my face as I watched him make his way toward me. He was dressed in all black sporting a nice expensive looking suit. He was wearing some designer sunglasses, and holding his black fedora hat in his hands. The last time I saw Wes, he had a nice mustache going on, now he was clean shaven. A look I was not sure if I liked just yet.

Wes extended his hand to me, offering a friendly handshake. It was funny. Back in the day we had this little hand shake we did. I would clasp wrists and grip his shoulders. Now he offers me this boring old fashioned hand shake. I accepted his gesture of friendship reluctantly.

"John. Its good to see you old friend." I gave Wes the old stare down before I replied.

"What?" he asked. Unsure and then realized I was looking at his garbs.

"These old clothes? Come on, I'm here undercover for Christ sake, give me a fucking break John." I nodded slowly.

"Undercover for who?" He looked at me as if I should already know the answer.

"Who do you think John. The mayor of course." I gazed around the area. He took a step up standing next to me, also looking around as he played with the rim of his hat.

"So what brings you here John?" I did not look at him.

"I'm just checking things out." Wes shifted his weight from one foot to the other.

"I see. Well I can assure you. I am in total control on this island. There's not a goddamn thing that could go wrong today." This was not the Wes I remembered. The Wes I remember was not this serious.

"So Wes…What's up with these fucking clothes anyway?

I mean come on you look like a fucking white collar asshole." he giggled a little looking at his own shoes.

"Yeah, well like I said, I'm doing some work for the mayor, and he likes his men to look top dollar. Know what I'm saying John?" I stopped for a moment to gather my thoughts.

"Yeah. The asshole likes to spend money on useless crap. I know." He giggled a little more.

"Yeah. You of all people should know about the mayor's spending habits John." He said. I turned and looked at him with a little anger towards my former partner.

"What's that supposed to mean Wes?" He dusted off his cuffs.

"Well you know. He's spending all this money on useless secret programs and all. I mean its really sad if you think about it. Here you have a man with all the power in the city, able to do whatever he wants, or whoever he wants, and he blows it all on useless ideas. And sticking his nose were it does not belong."

I stopped and thought about everything Wes said. Judging by the tone of his voice, I could tell there was a bit of resentfulness towards the mayor. Obviously towards the fact that he spent so much money on the assembly of me and my team.

"Do I detect a hint of resentfulness Wes?"

I looked at him head half cocked down, arms folded in wait of an answer.

"It really doesn't matter anyway John. You see the work I'm doing for the mayor? Well, lets just say it's really going to change things around here." He placed both hands in his pockets not looking at me still gazing around the crowd.

"Things what things?" Wes turned his head slowly towards me with a great look of seriousness in his eyes.

"Things John. Its going to change things. You ask too many questions. Its going to change things, and that's all you need to fucking know."

Suddenly the man I was talking to was no longer the man I had spent fifteen years with as a partner, but a mere image of his former self. This was not the Wes Adams I knew. The guy I knew could joke around and would have been more excited to see his old friend. This man certainly was not the same man I used to know.

"I see, seems like things started changing already. So when did you become such tight ass Wes? I see you sporting this fucking suit. Talking about, me working for the mayor is going to change things. I thought we were pals. Aren't you happy to see me? I mean come on man, its been four fucking years...we were partners." He turned around and got right up next to my face.

"Look John. I have a job to do, and so do you. Can I give you a piece of advice? Forget all the bullshit you think you know, cause you don't know, okay? And I'm only going to say this once cause we were partners, and friends, so listen close, and pay attention. I suggest you take cover cause there's a *storm coming*. Get what I mean?" But I didn't get what he meant. Wes had changed so much in four years. And to meet here, like this, under these circumstances.

Wes extended his hand for a shake. It was another old fashioned one, nothing to memorize. "Whatever happened to the old handshake?" He still held his hand out, never taking his eyes off mine.

"Times change, people change. I have to go John." I swallowed my pride, and bit my tongue. I accepted the handshake from an old friend.

"Okay. Watch your back Wes." He gave a quick nod and began walking away as he talked and did not look back.

"You do the same John. Oh, and remember what I said, take cover." He disappeared into the crowd.

A security guard came running up along side me panting and leaning down holding his knees. "Damn. How do they do that?" I looked down at the sorry excuse for a security guard.

"Do what now?" I asked. He was slow to reply. "Getaway like that." I was confused. But this wouldn't be the first time today.

"Man are you a fucking cop or what? He was one of them. One of them assholes in black coats." He stood up slow.

"Except he didn't have a black coat on. But I know he was one of them." I dismissed the whole thing. I know Wes was a little different. But whoever these guys are that he was referring to I'm sure it was not him.

"That was Wes Adams. He's an old friend of mine." the guard looked at me placing one hand on my shoulder.

"Look I don't care if he's your fucking grandma. That was one of them." I wiped the sweat from my eye.

"Dude. Please tell me what the fuck it is your talking about?" He cleared his throat beating his hand to his chest.

"Well I haven't figured out who they are, but I know them guys are up to something. I have been chasing them all day. Some suspicious people they are." I remembered all the little rumors I have been hearing lately about the men in black coats. I dismissed them all. Nothing more then the paranoid delusions of tabloid fucks.

"Your fucking nuts man. Your letting all that bullshit you see on see TV get to you." I shook my head as if I pitied him. He frowned and started to walk away.

"Believe what you want officer. But I am getting down to the nitty gritty here." My instinct told me to let him go, after all he was just a crazy rent a cop, but after seeing that clown guy, I guess I should believe anything.

I chased after him through the crowd. He was making great head way for fighting a crowd of this magnitude. I tried crying out to him.

"Wait. Hey wait!" It was no use he was moving faster I could only make out flashes of the back of his head. He jumped up atop of a stone planter trampling through the flower bed to avoid the crowd. I soon did the same getting dirty looks from flower lovers. He bumped into a trash can knocking it over, this slowed him down enough to get right behind him.

"Officer it's a fucking conspiracy. I have to find out what is going on. Now you can either hear what I have to say. Or you can fuck off. No offence." I was running out of breath, this man had the lungs of a teenage boy. Or he was just that determined.

A little boy came running ice cream in hand, not even paying attention, he ran right into the leg of the security guard splattering ice cream all over his black slacks. It was this, that finally made him stop and lean down towards the now crying little boy. He offered a friendly pat on the boys shoulder at a futile attempt to console him. But to no avail the boy just cried louder then before now calling out for his mother.

I stood over him as he still attempted to calm the boy down. "Alright, you win. I will hear what you have to say." I was out of breath, sweat dripped from my brow and my bullet proof vest felt as if it weighed a hundred pounds. "But make it quick. I have shit to do."

Standing there listing to Greg's story.(which is who he introduced himself as.) seemed to bore me. He would babble on about government conspiracy's, and cover ups. And how he chased these guys dressed in all black all over this island. When I questioned him why he never called for back up. He blatantly ignored me, and simply continued in his rambling. I was wasting my time with this guy I thought. I should be checking out the area. Not listening to the endless chatter, of some crazy ass island patrol guard, though part of me thought he could have a point. I remember what Jackie was saying in the chopper.

I heard the mayor's announcement. The speech was over and now he was to christen the ship. I told Greg to shut up, he stopped without hesitation, something I wish I could teach Bobby. I turned around to watch the christening. It was funny. I had this feeling that I had to witness this, as if my whole life I had been somehow trained for this moment. Sometimes even in the heat of the moment my instincts will kick in and I'll drop everything I'm doing.

A crew of caterers dressed in white coats were pushing a cart with a metal bucket filled to the brim with ice. Peeking out the top of the ice was the head of what looked like a fine bottle of champagne. I glanced upward to the top of the ships hull. Bobby was positioned at the top looking down. All was silent as the mayor reached in the bucket to pull out the bottle. "This is it." He said.

"Time to christen two of our latest additions to Chicago." After a quick glance at it, he held it in the air for all to see. The crowd cheered with joy.

*   *   *   *

The Conspiracy

*   *   *   *

The Mayor pulled his arm back ready for the shatter. He had a stance as if this were opening day for the White Sox, and he was about to throw out the first pitch. I remember watching his arm swing down, it swung into oblivion. The madness began. That's all it took was one swift blow from the bottle and the entire ship exploded into the sky like an awesome Armageddon. How it happened? I don't know, but I remember the horror it brought. The huge cloud that formed over head, the loud booming sound it produced that danced and echoed in my ears, and continued to ring even now as I tell you this. All that were on the ship were incinerated, even Bobby. The blast caused fragments of the ship to fly in all directions. One sharp flaming silver piece flew through the air like a Frisbee slicing torsos in its path causing there severed bodies to split in opposite directions. The metal sliced through a man's neck sending his head through the air. Limbs, arms, torsos, heads. All flew through the air. Two men standing right next to the boat screamed in agony as there bodies melted away from the flames that engulfed them. Pieces of hot metal flew through the air impaling everything still standing. Through the heart of a woman, the head of a an old man, the chest of a young boy, even the stomach of a man.

The carnage was unreal. The huge anchor that was attached to the side of the ship flew through the air as if it had been cast like a fishing lure. It may as well have been, instead of worms, it used human bodies. Scooping them up as it flew still somehow attached to the ship through a chain. Six bodies laid on either side of the anchor. The anchor shattered the skulls of the ones it did not impale. The mast came down atop a slew of mostly all ready dead bodies. Blood and brains splattered the area, like a sea of spaghetti. Some still wallowed on the ground burning away, wallowing with out limbs. A man tried to crawl away with just one arm and nothing below his waist. A woman embraced what was left of her son balling in agony.

Thousands were dead, and somehow through it all I was lucky, Greg on the other hand was not so lucky. A piece of the ship flew through the air slicing his legs off at the thigh. He was still breathing which was more then I could say for the rest of these people. Blood drained quickly from his body, I knew he would not last much longer. I picked him up throwing him over my shoulder.

Smoke filled the sky causing my eyes to water and burn. Visibility was almost non existent. I looked all around for a safe place or help, but I was alone, almost no one that was out side during the blast survived. Bodies everywhere. It was a virtual sea of death. I reached for my Two-way radio.

"Mira can you hear me?" I heard nothing but static. I repeated myself and retrieved nothing but static. Suddenly I could hear something come over the radio. It was screaming. People were crying out in pain. Gun shots were being fired. Who was shooting? Was it Mira? And for what reason?

"Mira do you read me?" Now the static returned, no reply from Mira.

I could feel Greg's blood run down my back and pants. He was dying fast. I could not remember the name of our chopper pilot. I tried with all my will to remember but to no avail.

"Hey Porky? Hey if you're getting this. Get your ass back to the island now! We got a major situation hear." I stopped and thought to myself, what a prick that commissioner is. Giving us such cheap budget cut back pilots. I bet that fuck flew him self to a pub somewhere.

I tried an attempt to contact the Commissioner.

"Commissioner. We got a big freaking problem here on the island, and you need to get your freaking ass in gear and send some reinforcements. I got a body count here of well over one thousand, I'm pretty sure Bobby's...The rest of the team is unaccounted for." After a brief moment of silence the static was gone.

"John, slow down and think about this for a second." His voice was all raspy from years of smoking cigars.

"Think about what your implying, don't you think I know of this skirmish? I mean a man of my power should be on top of things right?" His pompous attitude was nothing new, I thought maybe in a situation like this he could express himself in a more respectable manner. This was not the case.

"Look commissioner. I got dead people everywhere. You need to hurry the fuck up! You may be my superior but I swear to God I will fuck you up!" Before he replied I could hear him take a puff off his cigar over the radio.

"Relax John. Sit down have a smoke. Oh yeah, I forgot you quit. That must be driving you insane right now." I looked at Greg. He was fading in and out of consciousness.

"Fuck you Commissioner!" I was done with him.

I laid Greg down on a nearby park bench, pushing off some mangled body parts on the ground. He looked up at me as with the last of his strength to move his eyes.

"John. I want you...to tell...everyone my story..." He looked down at his hand to the wedding band was on his finger.

"And tell my wife...I love her...and my children." With that Greg departed this world. Though he was gone I still nodded and said I would fulfill his dying wish.

CHAPTER 7

▼

12:37 PM
Nowhere to Run

He paced back and forth with his hands clasped behind his back. His head was facing down to the ground. His movement was slow and steady. He looked as if he were lost in great thought. Wes Adams, what did he have to do with all of this? It was clear to me know who he was, a soldier of sorts, a great man of the people, or so I thought once upon a time. I knew this man or at least I have met him on occasion. He was close to the mayor, a real ball buster. Now look what has become of him. A dreaded terrorist perhaps, or just another man with a vendetta against my now departed friend the mayor.

George had many enemies. But this man I never would imagined. I suppose I never knew him well enough other then he served the precinct for over fifteen years. As I sat there helpless hands tied behind my back still indulging the god awful stench of the rotting corpses next to me. The one that had been mounted to the wall in a crucifix fashion. I could only imagine what this man had in store for me. I thought about my poor wife. Did she survive the blast I wondered. Would we survive?

A knock at the door. A familiar voice, most likely one of those men. "Adams. I have word from Block." Adams opened the door, it was one of them. The one that shot the man in the sub level garage. He was dressed the same as them all in dark clothes, and a long black trench coat.

"Adams. Block sends word that he has received conformation of the assassination and will be arriving shortly." Adams nodded his head still pacing hands clasped behind his back.

"Does he know of the mistake?" What mistake I thought. It was an assassination just as I thought.

"No sir. I don't believe so. At least he mentioned nothing to me." Adams stopped breathing deeply.

"Alright, it will only be a matter of time till he does. In the meantime have all the remaining survivors rounded up and placed in the theater." The man in black looked puzzled.

"The theater, Sir?" Adams gave him a quick glance and turned his attention to me.

"What do you think Mr. Johnson? Wouldn't the theater be a good place to hold a few thousand people, all comfortable in there seats, perhaps even watch a movie." I was at a loss for words. Why was he asking me this?

"No answer, Mr. Johnson? Very well. Then, the theater it is." The man in black rubbed his chin.

"But sir, there are still a number of people alive. Shouldn't we just eliminate most of them. So we can maintain order better?" Adams turned around getting right up in the black coats face grabbing him by the sleeve.

"How many people were supposed to die today? Can you tell me that?" The man in black shuttered. For what reason I was uncertain.

"Only one, Sir." The man referred to him as Sir, could he be the one in charge of all this?

"And how many have died so far?" The man in black paused for a moment.

"A few thousand, Sir." Adams looked the man up and down. Still gripping his sleeve.

"Then you tell me. Should we just kill everyone and get it over with?" There was a cold silence for a moment then reluctantly the man in black replied.

"I don't know." Adams eased up on the man letting go of his sleeve.

"I'm a soldier, not a fucking terrorist, and what happened today has turned into an act of terror. Now put the hostages in the theater before we lose control." The man went for the door but paused and turned his head back to Wes.

"I have men rounding up hostages as we speak, Sir." Adams nodded.

"Good have them brought to the theater." Adams bent over gripping the handles on my chair. He was right up in my face. I could feel his breath on my skin as he whispered.

"Now Mr. Johnson. Your going to stay with me. I want you to witness all the horrible things your friend the mayor has brought upon this city. I want you to witness the corruption that has brought this day."

✶   ✶   ✶   ✶

12:57 PM
John Paddock and
The Black Coats

✶   ✶   ✶   ✶

What can be said of a man who didn't try? I tried. I moved from one body to the next. At least that were not obviously burnt beyond recognition or severed into a thousand pieces. I walked what seemed like a battlefield from the war. Carefully stepping my way between fallen casualties, not wishing to hear the crunch of a bone. I looked upon the carnage in hopelessness. There was no one. Not one soul left to save. I was either too late or the blast killed all. Alone, I made my way through the tragedy, with no contact from my team. The stench of still burning bodies making me nauseous. I felt as if I had died and this was my own hell. Maybe I did die along with the rest of these people. I wondered if I was just a wondering soul in search of my calling.

The sounds of machinegun fire and exploding grenades rung through the air. I looked all around and no one or nothing was insight. It continued to grow louder in my ear, I covered them with my hands, running through the sea of bodies, franticly panicking, and running from nothing more then fear. I dove behind a pile of bodies to avoid the shots, but there were no guns being fired, no bombs going off. Still I stayed behind this mass of bodies in hiding. Hiding from what? From my own failure, my inability to have saved these people before it was too late. I was no leader, I should have been lead. I shut my eyes tightly wanting the hell to go away, I forced the sounds of war out of my head, then a voice came. It sounded all too familiar, like my own. "John." Slowly I opened my eyes. A body that was not there before lay facedown in front of me.

"John." The body spoke to me.

"John." It said again my name. I breathed heavily the body began to move its head in my direction, it was my own face I saw, mangled and bloody.

"Welcome to hell."

I opened my eyes, I was standing there at the other end of the island, not effected by the blast, facing the skyline, where my nightmare was not. It had all been a dream, I really had been there inspecting bodies, but I had not encountered a dead form of myself, at least I hoped not.

I could slightly make out sirens, and lights. Though we were very far away from the beach. They gathered at the docks that led to the island. Finally, that asshole commissioner came through, I thought. At least that's what I'd like to think. He was a complete dick on the phone. Now my team and I, only had to wait for the Calvary to arrive. It would only be a matter of time. I had no idea where my team was. I lost contact with them during the blast. No one was around. Not a single man, woman, or child. Not a soul around. I wondered where they all could have gone to in such a hurry. Just as I was contemplating, I noticed some people swimming in full clothing out by the beach. They must have been on the island, but it was total ignorance to try and swim that far to the shoreline. They would certainly drown. There was nothing I could do for them.

A cool breeze swept over the island. From the lakefront breeze maybe, or from the approaching storm. Neither was a concern of mine. My concern was of the foul man Wes Adams had become If he did in fact have something to do with this, it was my job now to find out. I could search the island looking for my team, but it was far too huge, measuring at a quarter the size of downtown. I would not even know where to begin. In the stadium, the cathedral, the grand dining hall, the enormous green house with tall and exotic plants perhaps? The list goes on. No, I would wait for my team right here. Funny something tells me my wait will be short lived.

It was right at that moment Mira appeared like a ninja from the shadows. She was right next to me. I stood there looking out upon the lake. My arms outspread over the railing. I was startled at first, she never gave me a second glance. Instead, she joined me looking out to the lake.

"So what do we do now John Paddock?" For some reason I expected a warm embrace. After all I thought she might be dead. Now here she is after the explosion, still alive. But of course she was a professional so why would she. I thought.

"We wait." I was at a loss for words, I knew that was not the answer she was looking for.

"John a lot of people just lost there lives, and all you can say is we wait, I mean what about the ones that survived? We could be helping them." I never turned my head to her still not wishing to look back at the tragedy that surrounded us.

"They were incinerated."

"Incinerated? What do you mean?"

"I mean the only life left burned to death, everyone and everything standing outside at the time of the blast was killed."

"You survived."

"I know…look I checked the area. No one survived." I swallowed. "The few that did, they died a slow agonizing death…War is hell."

"I'm sorry?" Mira asked.

"Nothing." I explained.

I walked backwards away from the railing, remembering the gruesome sight on the other end of the island. Placing my hands together I rubbed them slow through the fingerless gloves hesitating to continue our conversation.

"We are up against a man who is better than me. A man I fought along side of for many years on the force. I don't know exactly what he's up to, and if this turns into a hostage situation, we may be the only hope these people have." A pale look came over her face as she turned to look at me.

"Wes Adams? He's behind this? That's impossible." I cocked my head to the side looking down at the ground.

"Well I would like to think so. But all evidence at this time points to him. You know its funny, Mira, just before the blast I ran into him on the steps. And do you know what he said to me? He said you had better find cover cause there's a storm coming in. And you know, at that moment I actually thought he meant he was referring to the storm to the west. But he didn't…he didn't." She was obviously puzzled by my words. I knew all along something was not right about Wes. Her hand rested on her sidearm, as if I was a suspect in all this. I knew it was just her police instinct though, especially in this most distressful situation.

"But now I know. It was a warning to me that something was about to happen. Its funny cause that's how he has always been. That son of a bitch. He gave himself away. Could he really have been so careless?" I said almost laughing at the thought. She stood there motionless still in her stance.

"Or maybe he doesn't think your going to live to tell the story John." She said with no remorse. I realized this was no laughing matter.

Maybe Mira was right though. Maybe Wes Adams thought I would not live to see the sunset.

"Or maybe it was a cry for help, from a remorseful man. Somehow I can't see Wes as being the type to take thousands of lives without a bit of guilt. It just doesn't make sense." She gave me a nod and changed the subject.

"By the way, just incase your wondering the positions of your men, Chuck is on the roof and Jackie is on the other side attempting to help anyone he can, but now after what you told me, it seems futile." I was not sure how to react, I felt as if I should be doing more then just standing around at the end of this damn island, but what more could I do for a dead body?

I cleared my throat. "How did you know where to find me?" She looked at me as if I should know the answer.

"Because John. In a situation like this, I know your first instinct is to make sure back up is coming." She stopped and glanced behind her to the gathering flashing red and blue lights on the beach.

"And by the looks of things, it looks like they are."

Just as she said this it happened. In an instant, the flashing lights were stopped and replaced by a loud explosion. The area quickly filled with smoke and fire. Ambulances, squad cars, S.W.A.T. vans and fire trucks were thrown from the docks out into the waters. The entire area was engulfed in flames the same as the explosion just before. All of our back up had been obliterated, erased from the world like the people on this island. It was clear to me now that we were up against someone who had had taken into consideration every aspect of police procedure.

Mira and I lay there on the ground instinctively jumping back when the blast happened. She looked at me as I lay there. "What are your orders John Paddock?" The shock of the explosion settled. Rage consumed me.

"We're going to find Wes Adams." She slowly rose to her feet.

"John…I don't believe Bobby survived the blast." This was something I had also taken into consideration. With one less member of my team, we were even more vulnerable.

"I know." There was silence between us. Never before had I lost one of my own. Bobby was an arrogant asshole, but he was still a member of my team, and now he was gone. I had always taught myself to maintain leadership in a situation such as this and to place my emotions to the side, but I could feel myself slipping away. It was a feeling I had never felt before.

She looked at me with tears welling up. It was obvious that she held them back with all her strength. Mira cared about Bobby more then I cared to know. I had always been slightly jealous of him for that.

"Its not your fault John." This was not what I needed to deal with right now. I needed an escape for both of us. Something to take Mira and my own mind off of Bobby. I did not reply. I knew it was not my fault. Why in hell would it be? Mira must have thought I blamed myself.

Just when I was out of ideas, my way out came running along. My way out that is, was a man in a black trench coat and black fedora running into the mall swiftly. Without even a word to each other we immediately ran after him. It was pure instinct to follow, and in any case he was our only lead.

The entrance to the shopping center was red with two large rectangular windows on each side. We passed through the glass double doors simultaneously. Inside was a long hallway with wall to wall shops, eateries, and games. The floors were black and gray marble, which kind of clashed with the red wallpaper in my opinion. This was yet another section of the vast island I had yet to explore.

A crash of something being knocked over came from the left, inside the restaurant. It was psychedelic and futuristic with neon black lights flashing everywhere. Slowly we made our way through the eclectic restaurant. The lights flickered unlike those of a power shortage. These lights were meant to flicker. Tables were a mess riddled with food, and a few even turned over. There was sticky spilt drinks all over the floor. This was the scene of great panic. People who had been eating here not long ago had fled in a hurry. Weird music was playing in the background.

We made our way through the mess of spilled French fries and cheeseburgers. The sheer aroma made my stomach growl. The thought of picking up a fry or two and indulging in the grease made my mouth water with desire. It was a distraction I had to stop thinking about. Mira was creeping with her 9 millimeter, hand in hand in perfect police stance. Myself, on the other hand, held a 45 with one outstretched hand strutting through the mess like an all American bad ass. After all I am John Paddock. The fearless leader of a prototype police squadron.

The black lights caused Mira's face to remind me of my high school days. The purple skin tone she wore from the black light beams was tripped out. Sure I dropped a little acid before joining the force, but in our day and age who could really say they have not? You could easily ask at least five cops if they had done drugs before, and at the very least one will tell you the truth. When I say the truth, I mean all five of them dropped.

I stepped in a dried up puddle of sticky soda, the purple stuff that tasted like shit, it stopped me. As I lifted my foot from the puddle of purple goo it made a low ripping sound. Mira looked at me and cringed still not saying a word. Dead silence was the idea, but I just botched that. It was hard to maintain silence with a sticky shoe. We took a moment to look around the area surrounding us to see if our friend in the black coat noticed my little noise. But there was no sign of the man in the black coat or anything else for that matter. Only the mess that surrounded us, and the tripped out lights and music that caused Mira's face to seem to get up and dance.

We stopped briefly, I was wishing not to move my sticky shoe again, giving away our location. I looked at Mira, a single tear rolled down her cheek while she remained in perfect stance. I whispered.

"What is it Mira?" She shook her head and quickly wiped the tear away.

"Nothing Paddock." She called me Paddock, something she never does, its either John or my full name, but never just Paddock.

"I need you to be strong for me officer. There will be time for remorse later." I said. She replied with a quick nod and began creeping her way through the mess. I knew she was thinking about Bobby, and that was unacceptable. She knew the consequences when she joined the Secret forces. Once our team dies, there will be no record of this prototype secret force. All matters must be dealt without interference by the government or media. All matters were to be dealt with in a manner of ordinary police business. We are all disposable, and will be treated as such. Those are the exact words as they are written in the hand book. A book she knew all to well, following it to the teeth. Bobby knew this too, and paid the ultimate price.

The sound of the music was chilling. The air conditioning caused the sweat on my body to practically freeze like icicles in the winter time. With every step I took my boots would make a ripping sound from the sticky soda, Mira cringed every time she heard it. We passed under a round bowl like object suspended from the ceiling. The area was so dark it was hard to make out what lurked in the shadows. We were walking blindly. At any given moment this man would jump from his hiding place and take our lives. This was our first real situation of great importance since the Special forces rouge squad began two years ago. I was already out one man, and there was no chance of any back up any time soon. I'm sure these guys have discussed the hostage situation with the police already. I had no idea what they wanted. If the mayor really had to do with some conspiracy, then why did he let himself get blown away? All this ran through my head as we crept through the poorly lit Restaurant.

"Don't you have a flashlight equipped Mira?" the question sounded stupid, why wouldn't a member of the superior forces have a flashlight? If only I had remembered mine before we landed on the Island.

"No John. I would have had it out by now, don't you think?" She stopped for a moment and looked at me.

"Where's yours?" something startled me from the side, but I quickly dismissed it as my own imagination.

"I freaking forgot it on the chopper. How about you?" she sighed. "I lost it during the commotion." Then I sighed.

"Well that's freaking great. Here we are, walking blindly in the middle of a possible terrorist situation, without a freaking flash light."

Suddenly a round of bullets came from the darkness, hitting a table directly in front of us. I quickly wrapped my arm around Mira and pulled her down to the floor behind a condiment counter. A rain of bullets continued to spray the area. He was firing an automatic sub machinegun. For a moment I thought their could be multiple men shooting, but quickly dismissed the thought.

He fired relentless, not even easing off the trigger for a moment. "We need some serious fire power, if we even want to stand a chance against this guy, Mira." I was shouting over the sound of the gun. She nodded and was removing her radio from its holster. I looked at her with a bit of doubt.

"Your radio works? Before I could not get a hold of any of you, and what was the deal with all those gun shots?" She looked at me and glanced at my radio.

"I'll explain later...Maybe its yours that doesn't work John." I looked down at wires that protruded from a large crack running down the side of the radio.

"Good point." She cracked a small smile.

"I must have broke it when the ship exploded."

"Jackie come in, can you read me?" He came over the radio with that soldier attitude.

"What's the situation, Sir?" She held it tightly to her lips as if it were a phone.

"We are located in the psychedelic restaurant on the far west side of the mall. We need back up!" Suddenly the radio went dead.

"Jackie? Jackie come in. Fuck!" The gunfire ceased and only the sound of the music in the background was heard. Possibly our assailant was reloading, but more likely he was coming to look for us.

I could hear my heart beat from my chest, but it was only in my head that I could truly hear the beating of my heart. Mira was breathing heavily, holding her gun pressed tightly to her chest. This man was wielding an automatic sub-machinegun and there was no chance in hell I was going to exchange fire with my 45. All we could do was sit there and wait.

The sound of footsteps could only mean he was approaching us. The music played, making everything seem that much more surreal. I griped my gun ready to at least get a shot off before he blew me away. The foot steps grew ever closer, now sounding as if he were right on the other side of the condiment counter. This was it, it was all over. I looked at Mira who was already preparing for the worst.

Suddenly, out of the darkness annihilating the silence like a sonic boom, the windows began to shatter. It was Jackie, shooting through the windows of the restaurant, he ripped through them with his M-16 until all the windows were gone.

The man in black fell dead right next to me. His body riddled with bullet holes. Another second and we would have been the ones on the floor.

Jack stepped into the restaurant through the new opening where a window once was, stepping down onto shattered glass making a cracking sound. I was relieved and yet disappointed in him for his reckless behavior. From Bobby I would have expected this, but not Jack.

"What the fuck were you thinking? You could have killed us all!" He stopped, his face turned pale, as if he were afraid of me.

"I'm sorry John. I wanted to catch the guy off guard." I turned and looked down at the body that lay before me.

"Well I think you managed that." Mira was shaking as she slowly stood up. She turned and looked at Jackie, and back to me.

"Thank you Jackie." She said with a sigh of relief. Jack scratched his head in confusion.

"I'm sorry John, what else do you want me to say?" With a wave of my hand and shake of my head, I dismissed him.

"Nothing. Just next time be more careful. You pulled a stunt like that asshole Bobby would have." I said. Not the best choice of words I could have used, I'll admit. I looked at Mira, she was already wiping a tear from her eye, Jackie gave me a look of sheer disappointment.

"I apologize. That was uncalled for." Mira shook her head wiping the nostrils of her nose.

"Don't be John. We all know how you felt about him. There's nothing to apologies about." Her words were cold and emotionless. I knew she wanted to scream at me, but refrained because I was her superior. There was silence for a moment. Jack was spaced out starring into nothingness. He removed his hat placing it over his heart, lost in a prayer. Mira soon joined him, they stood there together in their prayer. I was uneasy and feeling a bit awkward, I exchanged glances with them.

"Lets all remember Bobby for the damn fine officer he was." I said. Mira just stood there. Jack exchanged glances with me and Mira.

"No. Lets remember every single person that died today, and never forget." Jack said. We all stood and joined in bowing our heads. To honor those who have lost there lives in a war they had no place in, is truly the greatest honor of all. They knew not of there fate today, it was to be a day of recreation, and then tragedy comes into play.

Jack was the first to place his hat back on. I was grateful for this, for I had no desire to be the ice breaker.

"John." He said. "Lets find these filthy sons of bitches." It was clear to me now that we were the only hope the surviving hostages had, and now was the time to act.

"Lets see if this stiff has any I.D. on him." Mira took the liberty of checking the body. He was an older man, I would say early sixties. With short gray hair and fair skin. His empty, cold, dead eyes were still open, glaring right at me in a haunting afterlife expression.

"One thing I will never get used to about this job is the stiffs." I said to Jack.

"The ones that look at you, even after they died. I don't know if you ever took the liberty, or even had the chance to look a dead man straight in the eye, but its one experience In life that will send chills down your spine, especially the ones you ice yourself." Jack nodded in reply.

"Hey guys." Mira interrupted. "I think we could be caught up in some something big here."

"I could have told you that." Jack said. Mira was knelt down looking up at us, holding her gun in one hand, and the stiffs wallet in the other.

"How serious?" I asked.

"This guy is government, I mean like Washington."

"Let me see that." I grabbed the wallet from her hand. The thought of killing a man who may or may not have been on our side gave me the chills.

"This is impossible. He's an agent?" It was all there in black and white, Arthur J. Wallace, F.B.I. Jackie gestured his hand down towards the dead body.

"Well he was an agent. He's kind of dead now." Jackie said. His eyes moved rapidly from mine to Mira's. He shrugged.

"So what does this mean guys. That I killed a fucking government agent?" Jackie said, as he grabbed at his hair practically ripping it out.

"Fuck, I'm going to fry for this." I quickly dismissed the idea. I would not let my team fall apart over a misunderstanding, especially after I blew a man's penis off earlier.

"Nothing like that Jackie, don't worry, I think this guy was just playing agent as a cover up." I had no idea really, but needless to say it was all I could come up with to calm Jackie's nerves. Mira interrupted me.

"Was he John? Or maybe all these guys are part of a big government conspiracy. You said yourself that your former partner Wes Adams was one of them." I rubbed my face with the entirety of my hand.

"I don't know for sure, I think he is, I don't know." Jack scratched his head in confusion.

"Look, both of you are confusing the fuck out of me. So which one of you wants to fill me in?"

"I need a cigarette." I said.

"What?" Mira asked.

"I said I need a cigarette."

"You quit."

"Fine then a Tylenol." I pulled a bottle of Tylenol from my pocket and popped three or four pills. Mira gave me a sidelong glance in disapproval.

"What? They make a great substitute. Plus they are non-habit forming." I looked at Jackie, he seemed to be in a stupor just staring blankly at me as I swallowed the pills.

"Do you remember how you were saying earlier that you think the street cops were up to something. Like they had some kind of deal worked out with the scum's?" He nodded in agreement.

"Well I think its bigger then just Chicago street cops." Jack looked at Mira and me with his jaw agape.

"You mean it's us versus the world?" I took a clip from my side slamming it in.

"Jackie. We may have just stumbled on to one of the biggest cover ups in history."

CHAPTER 8

▼

One Hour Past 12:57 PM Reserved Material
The Unholy Church of Modern Babylon

*　　　*　　　*　　　*

"And now, here in our darkest hour, in our darkest time, we all should know, that the end is upon us. But fear not! Brothers and sisters. For we remain protected under the sanctity of Gods hand."

*　　　*　　　*　　　*

The Preacher mans voice echoed through the beautiful gold and white marble Church. On some rarest occasions the stained glass windows would shake from the booming sound of his voice. Then again it was most likely nothing more then my own imagination. How could a man, even a man like this, cause windows to shake I ask? He cannot, servant of God he may be, but not even a servant of the almighty no matter how many times he may converse with him, has the ability to shake windows with the sounds of his voice alone. Perhaps he used some sort of control devise to cause them to shake. Either way, I knew it was impossible.

Many had taken refuge in this house of God, this manmade, self proclaimed supposed sanctuary. Young and old, various ethnics, rich and poor alike, all in one room. I found it difficult to believe that all these people were of the same faith, the same religious denomination. Most likely they were not, but in times of great terror and the fear of death can cause any man to turn to God in the final hour. Even a blasphemous man who has spent his days with a hatred for God may seek him out in the final hour.

The final hour? What a joke. I would rather be sipping a long island beside the pool typing away at my lap top as I am now. I was not a follower of God, nor was I an atheist. I guess to put it bluntly, God fucked me over as a child, and I have since found no desire to follow him. Now you may ask yourself, what is a man like this doing here in this grand church with an astonishing twenty foot high Michelangelo ceiling, and royal pillars that widen as they grow to the top swirling like a tornado, and a streaming fountain of holy water just behind the preacher man. No I have not found God in this dismal time. Nor do I believe in doing so he would save me, only a fool would believe such things. A lifetime of sin cannot be forgiven in the grand final hour. I am simply a man taking refuge from the carnage that swarms the outside. There I was, minding my own business, typing away at my lap top, when some ruffian decides to blow up that beautiful ship.

$$* \qquad * \qquad * \qquad *$$

"The lord works in many ways, ways that many can't imagine, or the few can't understand. Ways that would cause you to become like a crazy person if you were to try."

$$* \qquad * \qquad * \qquad *$$

His endless chatter made no sense to me. He was improvising, stalling the pending doom as it were. A lackluster attempt to cheer the hearts of many, or the few, or whatever the hell amount he was talking about. None the less, I have heard it all before. The Lord works in mysterious ways, I never understood the concept of that saying.

As I sit here typing, sending this information to my website. I realize that I have little time left. I continue to type ever frantic to achieve my goal in sending all the information I can dear readers. I know the future, I have foreseen my own pending demise. It's here today, on this island. It's only a matter of time now, dear readers. This will be my last entry to my successful dot com. I apologize to all my fans. I'm sorry and regret that I will never be able to publish the book I have worked on for the last three years, *The Fear of Decay*. Alas, I will leave this earth knowing that at the very least, you all will be able to experience a little of the hell that these men in black trench coats have brought upon me, at least in text, You will understand.

*   *   *   *

"Why do only the good die young you ask? Well I will tell you brothers and sisters. Because they are the most likely to reside along side of the lord himself in heaven. To become masters of His domain.

*   *   *   *

Ridicules I thought. What was he talking about? I stopped my entry for a moment to gather my thoughts, after hearing his sermon become more and more out of context and made up as he went along, still the nameless ones gave him amen's and hallelujahs. It will never cease to amaze me the human psyche. If I had more time, I would write about it.

I stop and wonder what would happen if not a single one of us lives to tell our story today. I only hope some will listen. I know by the time this all gets loose, the masses will deny it ever happened. I only hope that my fans who are reading this now, as I write at this very moment, reading every single word I'm typing, will understand that this tale of suspense has been told through the view points of those who lived it, in different perspectives. And I hope that others will follow in my foot steps and make known all that has and will happen today.

Just as I have foreseen, a dark and sinister fellow in all black has entered the sacred holy grounds. Entering through the doubled arch doors as if he were the king of this island and all shall bow before his royal prestigious being. He had a smug look on his badly scared face. One scar went right down his face diagonally from his forehead through his nose, down to his horribly scarred chin. He removed his sunglasses and gazed around the church with one blue eye and the other a milk white glass eye. Behind him, two more men in black trench coats entered, there heads low so only the tops of there black fedoras could be seen. Simultaneously, the two men in back closed the doors and took positions side by side, hands clasped in front, and heads low.

The preacher paused for a moment and continued as if their presences had gone unnoticed. But his voice was now a raspy nervous sound that cracked with every quote. The horribly scarred man stood just along side me, looking upon the preacher with an evil grin revealing a cut and mangled smile. Half of his lip was missing revealing a disgusting bit of flesh from an old wound that had healed badly.

*   *   *   *

"Now I ask of you brothers and sisters. I ask of you…no I demand of you! To help me in expelling this evil presence that has tainted our sanctuary!"

*   *   *   *

Not a single soul turned to notice the newcomers in black. Instead they sat and listened to the preacher man, with no idea what he was talking about. But I knew. I knew he was referring to the men now present.

*   *   *   *

"Please brothers and sisters. I need you to pray now, with me. All join and pray."

*   *   *   *

The crowd clasped their hands and bowed there heads in prayer. "Oh dear heavenly father. Please give all your children here today the strength they need to dispel this evil that has befouled us on this joyous day of relaxation and happiness. A day for all your children to enjoy the fruits of their labor."

A bellowing Amen swept the crowed in unison. With that the scarred man also gave out an Amen and slowly clapped with that sinister smile on his face. The clapping of the man in black had drawn the attention away from the preacher, as all turned their heads in confusion. A hush came over the audience as the man in black made his way slowly down the aisle towards the preacher.

*   *   *   *

"Brothers and sisters, I ask of you now not to fear the demons, the demons that have tainted our house of God."

*   *   *   *

As the preacher man continued to go on about expelling the demons, I couldn't help but notice that not a single person was in a state of panic, rather they embraced the end. Either that or their ignorance was so great that they had no idea the end was near.

If only there were an escape. But alas the stained glass widows were far to high and even if I were to escape where would I go? We are on a manmade island in the middle of Lake Michigan. All I wanted was to give my fans a birds eye look at the new Little Chicago isle. And now I have given them a first glance at my own demise.

The preacher man stopped as the man in black made his way up to the podium. There was dead silence throughout the church. The man in black stopped and starred at the preacher man. The preacher man knelt down on his knees and clasped his hands together, looking to the sky.

"Please God, forgive him. For he is not a sane man. Nor has he seen the light you shine upon thee." The man in the black trench coat looked down upon the preacher.

"Dear. Dear. Poor dear Brandon, how tainted you have become. Parading around in this ridiculous robe. Pretending to be something you are clearly not." The preacher closed his eyes tight praying under his breath, he briskly opened them as if he had an epiphany.

"Please Axe, I had no intentions of abandoning you, or the Black Coats." Axe? What a strange name I thought. How did this horribly scarred man receive a name such as this?

The scarred one known as Axe, removed a pack of cigarettes from his breast pocket. He proceeded to speak as he lit the cigarette.

"You know it's funny." He paused taking a drag.

"We should meet here, its kind of like Gods way of saying fuck you Brandon Sikes. Your going to hell no matter how much fucking redemption you expect to receive pretending to be a priest." The audience mumbled amongst themselves in confusion. It was rather curious.

"You of all people, a priest? You amuse me with your outlandish cunning Brandon. I may be a ruthless killer with the scars to prove it, but you…You on the other hand. Your nothing more then a blasphemous, child molesting, rapist, woman beating, murderer." The silence was broken, the audience was in an uproar over this distressing news. How surprising it must be to find out a preacher you looked up to and trusted was touching your little boys private parts behind your back? Oh wait. Never mind. Its' not surprising at all really.

With a look of final redemption, the preacher on his knees and hands clasped, looked up at Axe.

"God will forgive you." Axe looked down at the preacher as he drew a gun from his side, pointing it point blank at the preacher's forehead.

"I don't think so…nor will he you." With that the audience was silenced once more. Slow motion seemed to control Axe as he pulled the trigger. Fragmentation's of brain and skull sprayed the front row. A scream of horror came from a woman as her white dress was doused in red. The preacher man fell face first into the holy water. It was a disturbing sight to watch the water flow red from a statue of an angel holding a jug. In an instant of sinful defiance, the entire church malformed into a house of evil.

Even with the growing alarm throughout, I still sit here writing you this grim story. I was not oblivious to my surroundings, rather in total content with my own death.

Axe made his way down the aisle until he was standing right beside me. The two men in black lifted there heads to reveal they were not men at all, rather two beautiful woman. Beautiful in a diverse way most of narrow minded society would without hesitation frown upon. Their nose and brows were pierced, and three silver hoops pierced through their bottom lips, their eyes were a stunning light hazel with skin as pale as snow. There similarities made them twins in a sense.

Axe looked at the twins, and abruptly turned his attention to his cigarette, taking another drag. "Torch it." He said with a puff. The two woman exchanged glances, the one nearest to me spoke in a very low arousing voice.

"Torch it, Sir? But the fire will spread throughout the island?" Axe took another drag and with a sarcastic voice said.

"Yes I suppose it would. Pour the gasoline." He demanded.

The two woman pulled out two tanks of gasoline with an auto spraying nozzle from their backpacks. They started down the aisle spraying it all over the audience. A few people tried to escape, but were stopped by Axe who pulled out a shiny silver hatchet from his coat. One man attempted an escape but quickly had an open gash put in his neck spewing blood like a grass sprinkler. Another tried to attack Axe from behind, Axe quickly turned ramming the hatchet into the mans side, he held him up with it till he died in midair.

I will die soon, this I know. I only hope that I can continue to write to the bitter end. The two woman finished their task and ran back to the door. Axe took another drag of his cigarette which was now down to the filter. He turned and surprisingly looked me in the eye.

"These will kill you." He said with a hint of sarcasm in his raspy tone. And with that I was certain he would flick the cigarette and ignite the church. Instead he put it out on the door behind him. A bit of relief came over me.

Axe and his two women associates left through the door, not even a moments later, his arm peeked through the door with a fully lit book of matches. The matches were tossed onto the gas soaked floor. Immediately, the church was engulfed in flames. Screams of horror came from those burning alive. It was similar to the events that took place outside post the ship explosion. Why we were not taken hostage I don't know, but yet I knew all along I would not live to see tomorrow. What difference does it make whether they shoot me, or I burn to death. One way or the other, I knew this would come.

Now dear readers, I must embrace death as he greets me with his outstretched cold lifeless claw. The flames draw ever nearer. The doors have been locked, so there can be no escape. This is the end dear readers, my final entry. The pain is great, I feel the flames eating my flesh. My laptop has started to melt, I… -**FILE UPLOADED-**.

CHAPTER 9

▼

One Hour past 12:57 PM
No Negotiations: Is Now playing in
The Theater

The huge Imax screen featured an old time intermission advertisement to try to get people to visit the lobby and purchase refreshments. It played continuously, over and over. My headache was full blown from the agony, the same hotdog popcorn and soda, all dancing around like fruity fairies, jumping in and out of each other. The enormous Imax screen presented it in its true original format. All the cracks and black lines that split through the old footage were more then visible, they were an eyesore. It reminded me of my youth, as matter of fact this old cartoon was probably older than me.

The theater itself was designed much the same as an opera house, with four balconies, two in the back center, and one on each side high above the rest of the seating. The wall was trimmed with black satin drapes that seemed to flow like a small wave in the water. The seating itself sloped very steep to provide all in the audience with a great view no matter where they sat. It was almost frighteningly steep, as if one false step could send you falling to your doom. The padding on the seats resembled that of leather, but I'm almost sure it was imitation.

After a short time had passed, the theater was full with a capacity crowd. God knows what they have done with the rest of the hostages. Judging by the sound of gun fire and the screams that followed I can imagine they shot them and dumped there bodies in the lake. Sick, twisted, sadistic, men they are. The amount of lost souls was great. I pray for my granddaughter Mary, her life is all I treasure, my own I would give for hers.

There were men in black coats posted everywhere, At every corner, all heavily armed with everything from pistols to automatic weapons. Some had their sunglasses on, though it was very dark. How could they possibly see in the dark like that? There was something also peculiar about those coats they wore. In the theater, the temperature was regulated by air conditioning, so I can understand that, but outside the temperature had reached well over one hundred, and from the looks of things none had even broken so much as a sweat.

One of them was walking by on the outer stair. Mary and I sat in the last seats in the row closest to the man. He slowed his pace, one foot down a step at a time until he stopped. He was talking into an ear piece.

"Yes. All the hostages have been accounted for, except those in the church…your on your way now?…good. And what of the cop and his team?…I see. You know how upset Mr. Block and Wes Adams can get when there are mistakes. Understood." He said in a calm and collective manner. He stood there rotating his head slowly around the room. Even with the black hat and dark shades they all wore masking their faces, I could tell he was in his early thirties. He was a good looking man with a clean shave. It was a shame to see a young man with so much potential, who was more likely then not going to be killed today. Such a shame.

One of the hostages sitting in front of us stood. He was well dressed in business attire. The man was also good looking, but slightly overweight in the mid section. His hair was brown and looked as if it had been cut recently. He was well groomed to say the least. He wore a smile on his face like he was about to close a deal.

"Excuse me." He said.

"Excuse me, Sir. I don't mean to interrupt or anything, you seem like a busy man who knows exactly what he's doing. I like that in a man, it's a trait we do not see all that often in our society." The man in black glanced at him for a brief moment, then continued to scan the area.

"Get to the point." The man in black said sternly.

"Of course. You see my friend, I am a business man. I work at a large travel agency downtown. Well actually I shouldn't be so coy, I am the C.E.O. there."

"I could care less. What the fuck do you want?"

"Right, right. I have a business proposition for you. Perhaps if we could talk in private?" The man in the black coat shook his head slowly in reply.

"Of course not. Fine. Well lets see here. I can offer you a large sum of money. Just you, of course."

"How much?"

"Millions. Millions my friend."

"I'm not your friend, and what exactly do you want?"

"All I want is to be set free, and in return I will give you ten million dollars. Think about it, that dream home in Hawaii you have all ways wanted, the sports car you could only dream of before. All the woman and wine you could possibly want. Come on, I know you feel it. So what's it going to be?...I think I know your answer." The business man smiled cocking his head down.

"I don't think you do." The man in black drew a nine from his side.

"Cause you wouldn't be smiling." He pulled the trigger, the business man went tumbling backwards down the steep stair, almost free falling just as I suspected.

"All of his money and all of his power, couldn't stop a bullet from ending him." The Black Coat said with absolutely no remorse in his tone as he stood there watching the business man fall to the bottom.

Mary started to cry, a man was just shot before her very eyes. Though it was nothing in comparison to the horror she had witnessed outside when the ship exploded, It was still traumatic. A girl her age, nor any girl for that matter, should have to witness such horror. Even if we survive this day, I know she will be cursed with nightmares for the rest of her life. The tears rolled off her cheeks like rain off a window in a storm. I held her tightly in my arms but still no comfort could be given. Oh, how I wished this nightmare would end.

Suddenly, the one whom they referred to as Wes Adams, came running along. He moved swiftly towards the other black coat. Without so much as a word, Wes Adams swung at the Black Coat, hitting him square in the neck. The Black Coat gagged, grabbing his neck with both hands as he fell on his bottom, landing on the step. He was gasping for air, his face turned red.

"Idiot! This is not the killing fields. This is a highly planned out professional operation. We do not go around blowing people away. You're a trigger happy freak!" The Black Coat continued to gasp as if his wind pipe hand been crushed.

"The plans have been changed Wes." A tall man dressed as all the rest, was now standing behind Wes.

"What the fuck are you talking about."

"You know, only the Mayor was supposed to die and a few innocent bystanders too close to the ship. Now that a little more than the Mayor and a few others have died, Block has changed the plans."

"Under who's authority?"

"His own."

"In what way?"

"Simple. Eliminate as many as we can. We don't need to be babysitting hostages. Having a few is plenty." Wes Adams looked frustrated as he removed his hat running his fingers through his hair.

"Son of a bitch!" Wes exclaimed for all to hear. Another man stood next to Wes Adams. This man however was not dressed in all black, rather dressed in a normal blue suit, all except the jacket was missing, he wore a white shirt and blue tie, with blue slacks.

"Mr. Johnson? Now you have witnessed what your friend the departed mayor, has brought upon these innocent people. Were it not for his ignorance, none of this would have happened. I told you I was going to show the horror that he has brought upon all these people." He gestured around to the hostages. "Upon myself!" He clutched his fist tightly to his chest.

"Most will die, and you will live to see it." Wes Adams looked Mr. Johnson right in the face.

"I would also like to apologize about your wife, as I understand she was quite dear to you…" He paused briefly. "and the Mayor." Mr. Johnson sneered grinding his teeth with great anger.

"If only she had been standing next to you like a good wife, rather then next to him…hand in hand." Wes Adams said with his back turned. Mr. Johnson looked as though he was ready to rip Wes Adams apart, still he refrained. "But I'm sure you were already well aware of there…well you know."

"What?" Mr. Johnson demanded.

"Affair."

"My wife loved me."

"Dwell on that Mr. Johnson. Dwell on the true hate you felt towards him, make him suffer in your minds eye. Indulge the anger. He was your so called friend. He was your hated enemy." Wes Adams said with great hatred. "I will not succumb to your trickery." Mr. Johnson said.

"So be it. Then you will execute them personally." Wes Adams said as he grabbed Mary from my arms. "Do it!" He screamed as he held his gun with Mr. Johnson's hand to Mary's head.

"Do it!"

"Pull the trigger, and watch her die."

"Admit to your hatred."

"No. I will not!"

"Then she will die!"

My heart raced, I could not bare this. I jumped from my seat. "No! Please, I beg of you. Take me."

Wes Adams looked at me and raised a brow.

"Alright." He said, as he took the gun away from Mary's head and aimed it at my own.

"No!" Mr. Johnson yelled. Wes Adams turned his attention to Mr. Johnson.

"It's true. I hated him with a passion." Wes Adams let go of Mary, she jumped into my arms.

"Grandpa I was so scared."

"I know dear, it's alright."

Wes looked at me. "That was a noble act old man. Something the Mayor knew nothing of." He said calmly.

"Old man. What is your name?" He asked. I hesitated. "Its Kenneth Gill."

"And the girl? Your granddaughter I presume."

"Mary."

"Well Kenneth, I can assure you, you and your granddaughter will be safe."

CHAPTER 10

▼

2:01 PM
The Storm

Jack was outside, in the area where the ship exploded, searching for clues. Chuck was on the roof just above us. Mira and I sat there in the dining hall in silence. Somewhere on this island was a madman, with a goal unknown. We had not seen a Black coat in some time. That was the nickname we had given them, "The Black Coats." It was fitting to say the least. Mira was upset over the whole ordeal, so I said we should regroup in the dining hall to gather our thoughts.

Mira and I sat there at a table with white table cloth, and some wine that we did not partake in, though the thought crossed my mind. "You know Mira. When I asked you if you had what it takes to be a Chicago special forces operative, you were all up and ready for the responsibility." I stopped and looked at her. She was playing with a fork, scratching little rips into the white cotton table cloth.

"I tried to warn you from the beginning that this day would come, things would get heavy, and the amount of casualties would be great." I said. She tore a huge rip.

"I need you to be strong. I know everything that's happened today is a great burden, but there are still a lot of people out there that need our help." A single tear rolled down her cheek, she nodded.

"You just don't understand John." She said.

"Understand what?"

"Nothing."

I wanted to understand, but I had a job to do and that was all that ran through my mind.

"What are you scared of John?" She asked. The question caught me off guard.

"Ompalumpa's." I said attempting to liven the situation. She giggled a little.

"No. I mean what really terrifies you?"

"Honestly. I can't say that I have ever really thought about it." I said. She looked into the fork as if it were a mirror.

"I'm afraid of dying John." I laid my head down in my palm rubbing my face.

"Not for myself, but for my daughter." I sat there and listened.

"What will she do if I die? Where will she go? Who will take care of her?" With a sad look in her eyes she turned to me.

"John, if I die…" I put my hands on her shoulders.

"Your not going to die Mira, I will make sure of that." She put her hands on my elbows.

"No. Listen to me John. If I die I want you to…" I lost control.

"Damn it Mira! We are the most elite team of law enforcement this city has. You need to get a fucking hold of yourself!" She looked as if she were ready to start balling her eyes out. With a sudden unexpected reaction she slapped me across the face.

"Asshole." I let go of her and quickly sat up. I glanced around the huge dining hall. She was right, I had been an asshole. She was trying to tell me something and I blatantly ignored her. How can I expect to hold my team together when I constantly undermine them? She wiped a tear from her eye and sobbingly said.

"I apologize, Sir, I was out of line." I dismissed it.

"No apologies needed, it was my fault, I had it coming…what were you trying to tell me?" She shook her head.

"Don't worry about it, Sir. It was foolish anyway." I knew it was not. Yet I left it at that.

"Boss man! We got a fucking situation here!" It was Jackie. He was screaming into the radio.

"Remember that guy from earlier that was hanging out on the breakers? Well, I think I know what he was doing now." Mira and I exchanged glances, our guns drawn we ran out the door towards Jackie.

*   *   *   *

Intervention

*   *   *   *

He was standing at the end of the island, looking out leaning over the railing. We quickly made our way through the sea of carnage from before. The only way around the mess was to stay focused, look forward and never down, I only hope Mira was doing the same. She was so vulnerable right now, all she needed to do was step on a little girls head and that would be that, that would be the end of her stability, and perhaps my own.

It was beginning to rain, the storm hand finally made its way here, dark clouds lingered over head, the temperature had dropped by at least twenty degrees. A crash of lighting broke the water; a roll of thunder from behind, the sound was deafening. Although the drop in temperature was nice, the rain hitting my face was not.

Jackie was looking out into the choppy waters through binoculars. "What do you see?" I called out. He kept his focus without reply.

"What is it, Jackie?" I said as I stood next to him. He slowly removed the binoculars from his face handing them to me.

"See for yourself." I grabbed the binoculars from his hand. What I saw took my breath away. Slowly one by one with in a ten foot radius, the breakers were exploding with short intermissions between each explosion they swiftly made there way towards a tall old, white light house at the end of the breakers.

"What the fuck?" I said. That was all that popped into my head, what the fuck? I thought. I mean this is ridicules. Why was Wes taking out the breakers? Mira looked at me.

"John if those explosions make it to the lighthouse, we are in trouble." Jackie interrupted.

"Not to mention the lighthouse guy." He turned and looked at me. "He's fucked." Jackie said.

I looked at the lighthouse and thought for a moment. "Jack is right, if the explosions reach the lighthouse the keeper will go down with it."

"Quick Mira. Do you remember the lighthouse frequency we used back when we had that mission with the Cubans?" She stopped and wiped rain from her eyes.

"Yes." The explosions were growing nearer, they were visible now without the binoculars. Mira franticly changed the frequency on the radio.

"Attention lighthouse. Keep number three. Do you read me?" There was no reply, only static.

"Please come in. This is Mira Dontonelli, Chicago P.D. come in." The explosions grew louder, the sound of exploding rock and water echoed with every blast. The waves grew larger as the storm worsened. Rain fell more and more dense from the sky causing visibility to lessen.

An older mans voice came over the radio. "Yeah. What's up officer?" Mira gripped the radio with both hands as if it would blow away.

"Get out now! Jump if you have to! The whole lighthouse is going to blow." There was a pause and static.

"I'm sorry officer, I did not make that out, over." She shook the radio violently. The explosions grew close with only a few more to go.

"Damn it! Listen to me. The lighthouse is about to explode. You need to get out now!" There was only static.

I looked at the lighthouse through the binoculars. I could make out an older man peering through a window. The static continued with no reply. One explosion left till it reached the lighthouse. There was a crash of lightning that lit the sky. Another explosion and the breakers were obliterated, only the lighthouse stood.

Suddenly, something flew through the glass window the man was standing by. The man jumped through the broken glass falling far below to the waters. As he fell, the lighthouse exploded from beneath, sending it tumbling down like a chopped tree still in tact. It hit the water with great force, causing a tidal wave effect. Shit I thought, as the huge wave grew that was heading in our direction. With only seconds to react, Jack, Mira, and myself ran back to the dining hall, the wave grew larger towering over the island like a blue and white wall. We ran inside the dining hall. The wave followed close behind. We ran through the hall to the back as the wave came crashing through the windows, shattering them on impact. Tables and chairs were swept away. The wave engulfed us. I felt as though I was drowning, my eyes were open but I could see nothing but water all around, I tried to take short breaths, but I choked. The wave was gone as quickly as it arrived, receding slowly down the sides of the island.

I found myself lying there, with my back to the floor. I was drenched from head to toe. I was almost disappointed I had survived again. It was fate once more, leading me to live to find out whatever it was I needed to do before I died.

As I slowly stood up I looked around, tables and chairs were piled up on top of each other in a cluster in the corner. Mira and Jack were standing up. I made my way towards them. My boots made a squishing sound as I stepped. It was less annoying then the sticky sound they made before. My gun and anything else I was holding was gone.

"Everybody okay?" I asked as I slowly walked toward them. Jack nodded as he squeezed water from his smiley face tee shirt that was peeking out from under his bulletproof vest. Mira shook water out of her nine millimeter.

"Yeah…my guns a little wet though." I glanced around the room.

"I don't even know where my gun is." Jack removed his gun from behind his back.

"How's that old school machine gun of yours doing Jackie?" He studied it as it rest in his arms.

"Not good, another casualty of war." I ran my fingers through my wet hair.

"We need to find Chuck and get some weapons from him. I know he has an arsenal." Mira looked at me chin up.

"How about we contact the commissioner and find out what's going on." I shook my head.

"No good. I'm sure he's doing all he can." Mira raised a brow with a frown.

"Bullshit. You know as well as I do that asshole is not doing shit." I pointed a finger at her face and with a stern voice, I replied.

"Your out of line officer. He may be an asshole this I know, but that is our superior." She loaded a new clip giving me the look.

"Begging your pardon, Sir, but you and the commissioner can fuck off. I have a job to do." She looked at Jack, he was rubbing his gun, caressing it like a woman.

"C'mon Jack. We can handle this ourselves. Are you with me? Or our you going to keep taking orders from this incompetent arrogant ass?" I was shocked and at the same time vaguely expecting her sudden change of heart. Of course, I should have known this would eventually happen. My sudden mood swings and bipolar attitude could drive anyone to drink.

"Incompetent is it?"

"Yes."

"And what brings this on?"

"Years of waiting for something more, and receiving less." She said calmly.

Jack exchanged glances with Mira and I. Our eyes remained fixed on each other. I knew what she meant. Deep down inside I understood it was a deeper repressed expectation she had for me, and I let her down. I looked at Jack taking in a deep breath I asked him.

"Yeah Jack, what's it going to be? You going to follow an asshole like me around for the rest of your life? Or follow someone who knows where she's going?" Jack lowered his head scratching the top. Mira with a stern look said.

"If not I can take care of myself thank you." I shook my head slow folding my arms.

"No. Jack will go with you." She gave a quick nod and started for the door. Jack gave me one last look of dismay and followed her. I looked away from him. They we're gone. Everything was falling apart today, and now my team has fallen apart.

*   *   *   *

Mr. Cuban

*   *   *   *

I found myself walking outside in the pouring rain. I knew I had a job to do as well, but I didn't care at this point. As selfish at seems, the only one I really care about thinks I'm an incompetent asshole. Maybe I am a fraud. Who am I? The leader of this great law enforcement team? A team that no one knows of or could give a fuck about.

I remember it like a dream, something surreal and manifested into the realm of reality. It was two years ago, I had just successfully completed a big mission. We tracked a four time serial killer to his home on the southwest side. It was a heart pounding raid that consisted of Jack and I sneaking up the stairs and blowing the guy away before he had a chance to reach for his gun.

More then fifty men were posted outside, but all it took was two, just Jack and I, homicide detectives of the ninth precinct. Wes Adams was waiting outside, he was the head of the whole operation, and voted most likely to be promoted, or so I thought.

After the mission was a complete success, I was summoned to the commissioners office for a little surprise visit. At first I was nervous having no idea what to expect, but soon that aroma hit me and I became relaxed. It was a smell I knew all to well.

I remember walking in, I was engulfed by the distinct aroma of a burning cigar, the room itself was so clouded with smoke, visibility was not an option.

With a mix of gray and black I made my way through the thick smoke screen. It was the same as it always was, the commissioner would sit on his ass behind the desk puffing away at a big fat Cuban, and give out orders from his ergonomic, reclining, leather office chair. Always arriving before anyone else and never leaving his office with out his cigar in mouth and a big cloud of smoke around his head. This is how he received the nickname Mr. Cuban. No one really has an accurate description of him, other then the cheap suits he wears to mask his greatly large beer belly. I myself cannot remember a time when I saw the mans face, It was always masked by the thick cloud of smoke that seemed to follow him everywhere he went. Sure now and then you would see patches of his face, an eye here, an ear there, but never would you see the whole thing, it made him like a comic book character.

The man of course smelled something awful…awful disgusting that is. I knew he bathed on a regular basis, after all he would brag about his fucking Jacuzzi all the damn time. So I could only imagine he at least tried to practice good hygiene manners. Still that stench of rotting tobacco surrounds him always, no matter what he does.

I found the chair somehow through the thick smoke. It made a little creek as I sat, I knew it had to be leather, I started to cough a little, I had quit smoking about six months ago, and this was more then even a chain smoker could handle. Through the smoke I could make out a pair of lips and a bright, red cherry that grew brighter as he took in a drag. It was not a good idea to inhale a cigar as I have been told. But of course Mr. Cuban AKA the commissioner, would inhale like a hippie smoking a joint.

I cleared my thought's attempting to break the silence. The commissioner always waited and took a few puffs before he would speak, I could here the sound of a chair creaking backwards, with a raspy voice he finally spoke.

"John. Thank you for coming on such short notice…I know you have been all tied up in this case, its good to know its all over." He took another puff, I waited patiently without a reply.

"John I've been doing a little research, mainly on you. You see I have this…" He paused for a moment. I could tell he was moving in his chair, and taking another puff.

"…This new top secret idea. Do you know what this city lacks John?" I thought about the question a moment. I wondered if I was even supposed to answer.

"No sir, what does are fine city lack?" He took another puff.

"Good cops, John." What exactly was he implying I thought. Maybe I'm up for a promotion.

"Good cops is what this city needs more of. There is just not enough to keep the city safe. I've been working with the mayor on this new project for the past several months. We need a team of covert operative special forces." Did he want my advise? Or was he speaking in circles?

"Five people. One job, to protect and to serve this city like it never has been before." I coughed more from the ever building cloud.

"I don't understand, Sir. Do you need my advice?" I could see his hand come down from the cloud and extinguish his cigar. As soon as it was out he opened a drawer on his desk pulling another one out. As he loped off the tip he continued.

"I don't need your advice John. I need your help. I have already recruited four other people perfect for the job, but I need a leader." He lit the cigar with a torch lighter slowly turning it between his lips.

"I need you John."

I tried to adjust my eyesight to the smoke but to no avail, they were red and watery. "I need someone I can trust. Someone I know will be there when the odds are against him. I want you to be the leader of my elite special forces unit." It was like a dream come true, except for the fact I never dreamt about it.

"Pardon me, Sir, but I have a few questions before I take on that great responsibility." I said.

"Continue." He replied.

"First of all, who would be on my team?" For years I have been partnered with Jackie and Wes Adams was always our back up.

"Well, Jack Brown, of course." I let out a low sigh of relief.

"Who else?" He took in another puff and let it out.

"And Charles Jackson of the third precinct. You remember him right?" I nodded, though I know he could not see through the smoke.

"And two others, Robert Host and Mira Dontonelli." The name Robert Host struck my head like a lightning bolt.

"You don't mean that asshole rookie Bobby Host who transferred here from New York do you?" He leaned back in his chair.

"The same." I scratched my head in contemplation. "Alright, I can live with that…" Not really.

"Who's Mira Dontanelli?" He took in a puff speaking with the smoke still lingering in his mouth.

"Oh, you'll love Mira. She's a beautiful young Italian woman from the North side, just transferred here. Keep your hands off her. This is completely professional, got it Paddock?" He acted like I was some kind of womanizer.

I took into consideration all of what the commissioner said. Those people all sounded great and I'm sure the commissioner would not fuck me over with some low grade rookies, even though Robert Host was a New Yorker.

"I don't quite understand all this yet, Commissioner…" He interrupted me.

"Call me Mr. Cuban John." I shook my head dismissing the ludicrous nickname.

"That's okay, Sir. I will just stick with the Commissioner." He took a drag.

"Whatever. Anyway, John I know this is all kind of sudden but, well you see have you heard of the Block." Mr. Block alias the shifty chief. He was indicted on seven counts of fraudulent behavior. At least they tried to get him on fraud. Never proved shit, but the Mayor wanted him out of the city. A mutual agreement was made that he would never return to Chicago.

"Of course I heard all about it. He was banished from the city for fraud." Mr. Cuban the commissioner was digging through a desk drawer. At least that's what it sounded like. With all the smoke it was hard to tell.

"Take a look at this intelligence report." He handed me a print out I could not even read the first three letters through the cloud. "I cant read this, Sir." I said hesitantly.

"What the fuck kid? Go stand over by the fucking window." He exclaimed as if I were speaking like an ignorant fool, which I was. I walked over to the small office window it was tinted yellow from tar and nicotine. The Intel report read in courier typeset.

CONFIDENTIAL TIME SENSITIVE MATERIAL

Intelligence report:
OPERATION CO-WORKER
May 3rd 2003 13:34 Hours

Reports have been made that one Mr. Block former chief of police, has been rallying with the Cheng Sun clan. A full arsenal gang of libertarian weapons experts from China. Intel reports that the Cheng Sun clan has control of a vast arsenal of dirty bombs they have been harboring since 9/11. Word of what they intend to do with said weaponry remains unknown.

END TRANSMISSION

I stopped reading. "What does all this mean, Sir?" He took another puff.

"Simply that Block and the Cheng sun clan are making plans of mass destruction. No one knows the exact whereabouts of either. We do know they reside somewhere in Michigan." The idea of an American attempting an act of terrorism was repulsive.

"John…I have a strong feeling that he has a plan to attack the city." I placed my hands behind my head leaning back in the chair.

"I'm giving you six months to train and prepare your team. You will have all the funding you'll need. Just remember John, you and your team are expendable and at a any given moment something goes wrong. I don't know you. The Mayor don't know you. The precinct don't know you. The whole fucking city don't know you." I was given 24 hours to decide. I excepted.

*   *   *   *

Scar Tissue

*   *   *   *

I stood there on the edge my arms resting on the railing. The rain pouring down on me in heavy drops. The sky was dark gray and threatening. It made a face of evil looking down upon me, with lightning bolts shooting from its eyes. Was I such a bad leader that Mira had turned against me? Maybe she was just giving me time to situate myself? I was not sure who needed a grip more, Mira or myself. I thought about all that the commissioner taught me. I thought about Mr. Block. Was he really the one behind all this? These men in black did not seem to look anything like what I pictured the Cheng Sun clan to look like. Maybe the Cheng Sun clan had nothing to do with it. Maybe Block had nothing to do with it. The man Jack killed earlier, the Feds, what was his involvement? Maybe he was undercover? No, impossible it had to be something else.

I heard a sound from behind me. Not the sound of rain drops, the sound of footsteps. I swung around, gun drawn. There was darkness and nothing more. Get a grip, I thought. Then suddenly a bolt of lightning lit the night sky and revealed a horribly scared man next to me. He kicked the gun right out of my hands with one foot and kicked me in the face with the other. I flew to the side landing on my arm, my head bounced off the hard cement walkway breaking the skin causing blood to flow from my scalp. The man picked me up by my jacket.

"Ah, we meet at last, the infamous John Paddock, the one who would destroy us." He head butted me I dropped to the ground. He stood over me with a disgusting grin on his face. He grabbed me by the neck and punched me in the face three times, blood splattered the dark wet air.

"John Paddock, don't you even know who you are?" I spit out blood from my cut mouth.

"I know I'm the guy about to fuck you up!" He kicked me in the stomach causing more blood to fly out of my mouth.

"Do you even know what your purpose is?" I reached down by my leg grabbing a small knife from my side. I reached up and stabbed him in the side of his thigh. The knife stuck I could not remove it. It was as though it had no effect on him.

"Pitiful. After years of training and your nothing more then a clueless, mindless drone." He removed the knife from his leg with no more then a slight grunt.

"Then there's no point in you living. You have no idea the real reason you're even here today." He took the knife and stabbed me in the side of my thigh. I cried out in pain.

"I have been stabbed, slashed, and or cut 317 times John Paddock. Do you really believe that little knife could stop me? They call me...the Axe. Not because of my scars John, but because of this." He reached behind his trench coat and pulled out a small silver hatchet that shined when the lightning lit it.

"How do you know me?" He threw me against a stone trash can. His strength was great. He was a fairly large man. The hatchet shined as he played with it in his hand like a toy.

"Amazing the things people think they know, when they know nothing at all." I ripped the knife out of my thigh grabbing my leg in pain trying to think and slow the bleeding.

"What a shame. You will die knowing nothing. Always believing what they tell you to believe. Ignorant drone." I looked up at him.

"They, who's they?" I asked. "Why the media, of course. Filling the American people full of lies; never revealing the real truths, the real terror that lies behind a concealed curtain of deceit. Their are those who pretend to run this country...and there are the hidden ones who do." I took in his words. What could he mean?

"I know who you are. Your nothing more then a terrorist thug." I said with rage in my voice. He let out a low laugh.

"Then you truly don't know why you're here. I'm far from a terrorist John. You would be surprised how much we have helped this country."

Now was my only chance, his back was turned, I rose swiftly to my feet grabbing him from behind, clasping his arm with the hatchet twisting it behind his back. He dropped it swinging around twisting my own arm flailing me into a turn style. I regained my balance as he reached down for the hatchet. He lifted it to the air and threw it towards me. It came streaming through the air like a helicopter blade spinning in a circle as it sliced through the rain drops splitting them into two. It was on a direct course for my head, I leaned backward the hatchet flew over me. Less then a millimeter from my face it literately sliced the two day goatee off my chin bringing new meaning to the term close shave.

The hatchet hit a tree behind me wedging itself inside. Axe paused and looked at me I turned my head to the hatchet. I quickly turned around and removed it from the tree. I flung my arm around releasing it like a discus in the Olympics. It flew back towards him in the same manor it came to me. This time stabbing him in the side. He looked at me with hate in his eye, his jaw clinched revealing his yellow and blackened teeth. With great anger he spoke.

"Mindless drone." He turned and disappeared into the storm.

CHAPTER 11

▼

3:17 PM

"Hush little baby don't say a word, mommas gonna buy you a mocking bird, and if that mocking bird don't sing…"

"Shut up old man with that fucking singing." I gave the Black Coat a mean look as I held Mary tight to my chest attempting to put her to sleep.

"I apologize. My granddaughter is exhausted from all this excitement. I'm trying to put her to sleep." He eyed Mary up and down.

"I'll put her to sleep old man after I have a little fun with her first." He said that of a child molester which only made my skin crawl. Until now I have refrained from showing anger to these tyrants, but when it comes to my granddaughter that is something different. I gripped my fist tightly turning my knuckles red.

"If you touch her I swear I'll kill you." The Black Coat pointed his gun at my head.

"Fuck you old man." Another Black Coat came up along side him.

"That's enough. Go take a break, have a smoke." He lowered his gun and returned it to his holster under his jacket. The other Black Coat holding the AK-47 reminded me of a young Robert DiNiero. He had a calm attitude and seemed to be the only one of these men that had an ounce of compassion.

"Grandpa, I want to go home." I gave her a kiss on the head.

"I know dear, so do I. This will all be over soon, I promise." She raised her head to me.

"I miss my mommy, and my dolls, and my friend Amber, and my drawings, and my pet turtle." She pouted when she mentioned her turtle, it was the turtle I bought for her on her birthday. The one she saw at the pet store and told me she loved him so much and wanted to take him home with her.

"Do you remember how I promised I would get that turtle for you." She nodded.

"Well I did, didn't I?" Again she nodded.

"Well now I'm promising you that soon we will go home and you can see him again." She put her head back on my chest.

"Thank you, Grandpa." I rubbed her back a little.

"Your welcome dear."

*   *   *   *

Double Barrel
Mossburg
Spas

*   *   *   *

*   *   *   *

Ladies and gentlemen! Live from the windy city! Welcome to another exciting episode of the Chuck Man Show. Bump bump, bada bump bump. Yeah! Thank you! Thank you! Alright! Welcome to the show!"

*   *   *   *

Chucky had a small video recorder he kept in his jacket that he must have never told any of us about. Apparently, he used it to record the Chuck Man Show. A little dream he had always had about starting his own reality show on TV. A demonstration of the many adventures he has partaken in. Chuck was a guy who kept to himself, so it was no surprise to me to learn of his little show.

"Here I am again audience, caught up in another jam.

This time I'm right in the middle of enemy lines. I got maggots in black trench coats everywhere, I nicknamed them the Black Coats, I already took out three from the top of this building. Still no radio contact with the rest of my team, hope they okay. Anyway y'all still don't know exactly what the fuck I'm supposed to do other then scout this roof top."

From the view point of the camera, Chuck sat down on top of a ventilation shaft reaching into his pocket for chew. He started humming another one of those old tunes placing the chew in his mouth with the camera focused only on his face. In his right hand, he held a sawed off double barrel pump, strapped to his back was a Mossburg 590 9 clip, and a Spas 12 modified for optimum illegalness in the states. The barrel was short like a sawed off which was also illegal to civilians. It was Chuck's favorite.

He sat there looking up to the sky as the rain poured down on him turning his head to spit out chew.

"Aw sick man, you spit on me." Came a voice from behind, and suddenly out of the darkness it was Jackie and Mira.

"You need to think about taking up something less nasty, like smoking." Chucky let out a laugh as he rose to his feet to embrace his lost teammates. He wrapped his huge arms around both Jack and Mira simultaneously shaking them a bit. Jack looked down to the small video camera strapped to his chest.

"What's this, man?" Chuck looked down and back up to Jack.

"Oh, its nothing really, just for, uh, law enforcement purposes you know, don't need any Rodney King bullshit to happen, you know?" Jack rubbed his eyes.

"Whatever man. Anyway, you got an extra strap? All Mira and I got is her two 9 mm's." Chuck removed the guns from his back.

"Well, I got Mr. Mossburg, Dr. Spas, and of course, Sir, Sawed off. Take your pick." Jack looked at the rifles.

"Well, I think I'll go with the Spas. At least it's something like an M-16." Chuck shook his head.

"Man, you and that tired ass, weak ass, old ass gun. Anyway, I didn't want you to take the sawed off, she's my baby." Jack shrugged it off like a young boy.

"I don't know, I just like the classic physique of the M-16." Chuck shook his head holding out the Spas.

"Classic physique? Man, you want to talk about classic physique. Take a good look at this beauty." He held out the Spas with both arms like it were a baby, or an award. Jackie took the Spas with grace clutching it into his hand. The gun gleamed in the rain.

"Eh, I still prefer the M-16." Chuck rolled his eyes.

"Whatever, man."

Chuck glanced around the area, standing up on his tip toes looking over Mira and Jack. "So what the fuck? Where's the boss at?" Mira and Jack exchanged glances. Mira took the initiative.

"John…He went out solo to investigate and find the location of the hostages." Chuck gave her a look of disbelief raising one brow.

"Hostages? They got hostages? Fuck and I've been up here wasting my time." Chuck rolled his eyes.

"John was being an asshole again, wasn't he?" Mira lowered her head almost in embarrassment.

"It doesn't matter." Chuck shook his head.

"There's something you got to understand about John, sometimes he does not express himself in ways that others would find rational, but he always means well. Not only is he your commanding officer, but the only reason he lets you slide in areas that he would normally grill us for is because...well." Mira interrupted.

"Yeah, I know Chuck. He can just be so frustrating on and off duty." Mira stuttered for a minute attempting to say something, but the words would not reach her mouth.

"I mean, I have been trying to ask him to do something for me, but every time I do, the words just wont come." Jack and Chuck exchanged glances.

"What have you been trying to ask?" She shook her head.

"Nothing its not important." Chuck looked as though he did not believe her one bit, still he excepted it.

"Okay. If you ever need someone to talk to, I'll be here." She nodded, then Jack jumped into the conversation totally off key like always.

"Yeah...and me two." She looked at him and smiled.

Suddenly, out of the darkness a shot was fired hitting Chuck in the arm. He grabbed his arm wincing and cursing. Jack immediately had his Spas ready and began firing in the dark. Mira pushed Jacks arm down and grabbed him from behind taking cover behind a ventilation duct. Chuck was already hiding behind one across from them.

"Man, you two come up here for ten minutes, and already the peace and quiet is gone." He peaked around the corner firing off three rounds with his sawed off.

"Well at least your alive." Mira stood up quick over the ventilation shaft firing off six rounds with both 9 millimeters in both hands simultaneously. The target was nowhere to be seen, and these were merely shots in the dark. A few more shots were fired towards Mira and Jack. Chuck began whispering quietly into the small camera. "This is Chuck Man in the middle of real life gun fight between me and an unknown assailant." He peaked around the corner again.

"It would appear the assailant is firing from somewhere behind that chimney." Another shot was fired. This time in Chuck's direction.

"I have been wounded in the arm already, I'm going to make a quick bandage from my shirt sleeve." He said into the camera he ripped a piece of his sleeve off and wrapped it around the wound making a tight tie.

"Mira, I'm going to go sneak up from behind." Mira gave Chuck a quick nod.

"I'm sneaking in from the back now loyal audience." He said into the camera as he crept in low around obstacles.

Mira and Jack continued to divert the assailant with gun shots. Suddenly, there was silence and not a single shot fired from Mira and Jack, nor the assailant. Chuck stood still crouching down taking a quick look around. There was a flash of lightning revealing a figure running off the other direction. Chuck stood up letting out a few rounds. He then swiftly made his way in the direction of the assailant. Chuck crept up slowly to the body that lay before him. It was a another Black Coat, this one older, slightly over weight. Chuck held the sawed off in both hands aiming at his chest. He cocked it. There was no movement from the Black Coat. Chuck just stood with his gun cocked ready to fire. Then, without warning the Black Coat opened his eyes with a big grin his hand flew up towards Chuck, gun ready to kill. Chuck was quick having the advantage and fired four shots into his chest exploding it like a feather pillow. His lungs, heart and other organs were exposed.

Mira and Jack ran up along side Chuck. Mira looked at the body placing her hand over her mouth nearly stopping herself from vomiting, she coughed a little and cleared her throat. The coat began to spark and make a shorting out sound like a toaster that just had a metal knife dropped into it. They all had a look of puzzlement. Mira got down on one knee opening the coat.

"Its laced with wires?" She said looking up at Chuck and Jackie. Wires and micro chips were exposed through the torn jacket, little sparks would flicker.

"Help me get it off him." Chuck and Jack flipped the dead body over removing the jacket. Mira analyzed it. Sparks flew out little buzzing noises were made. Jack shrugged his shoulders.

"Well, what is he a robot?" Chuck looked down at the huge open chest wound he made.

"No. Undeniably not." Chuck said shaking his head slightly.

Mira tried the jacket on. It was three sizes to big for her, resting on her small body like a large blanket. Chuck and Jack both made disgusted faces because the jacket was covered in the blood and guts of the dead man.

"This is amazing." She said more to herself than to them.

"This jacket seems to adapt to any weather climate. As soon as I put it on I felt warm and dry as if it were not even raining at all." Jack looked down at the hat picking it up.

"Here try the hat on." She took it and placed it on her head.

"Just as I thought, its like a mini roof over my head." Chuck reached down and started taking off his black leather gloves. Jack took off his sunglasses.

"May as well get into the whole ensemble. Here try the gloves on." She placed the gloves and sunglasses on. She looked up to the sky with a huge smile.

"Wow! Guys this is incredible! This technology is amazing." She looked at Chuck and smiled.

"Well, what do you see?" She looked down at the gloves on her hands. "It's daylight and clear, not like night vision, but similar and ten times better. These glasses seem to be able to adjust to all weather conditions as well making it possible to see in the dark, rain, or whatever. And these gloves are just like this jacket, keeping my hands warm and dry." Chuck and Jack exchanged glances.

"That would explain why they keep attacking us in the dark. They can see us but we cant see them."

Chuck rubbed his head. "This is all very cool stuff and all, but we still don't know who they are or what they want? And what about the hostages, we got to find them." Jack said. Mira removed the gloves from her hands.

"No, we don't know who they are, but I know one man that does…he just needs to figure out that he already knows…and has known all along." Jack and Chuck looked confused and had no idea what she was talking about. Jack scratched his head.

"Are you talking about Wes Adams?" She removed the hat from her head letting it fall gracefully down onto the dead mans chest covering his putrid wound.

"No, the man I'm talking about is…officer Jonathan Paddock." Chuck dismissed the thought.

"What are you saying? John has something to do with this?" She shook her head removing the jacket.

"No. Nothing of the sort. I'm saying he knows something about them, he just doesn't know what." Jack aimed with the Spas turning slowly around in circles and said.

"Well, whatever, we still need to take these men in trench coats down…" He was interrupted by a woman's voice.

"We don't all adorn ourselves in trench coats, some of us prefer leather." It was one of the twins from the church. She was standing on top a square electric storage room. She wore an all black leather outfit with knee high black boots. The top of the outfit was like a corset tied in the back. Her ample breasts were half exposed by a half zip. Her hair was black pulled back in a tail. Another voice came and out of the shadows the other twin appeared.

"And were not all men." She stood next to the other hands on hips the same as her. The first twin jumped down on top Chuck wrapping her legs around his neck and knocking him to the ground. The other jumped down landing in a crouch. With a leg slide she knocked Jack down from under himself, the Spas flew out of his hand, she stood up and kicked Mira in the face sending her flying backwards. The first twin that was on Chuck had one knee on his chest, pounding his face into the ground with her fist. Chuck's camera flew over by Mira still recording. Jack tried to get up but before he could she kicked him in the face sending his head back bouncing off the hard roof, he was knocked out cold. She ran over to Mira who had her guns drawn, just as she pulled the trigger the twin was ducked down sliding foot first into Mira's stomach, Mira gagged grabbing her stomach.

The first twin stood up kicking the gun out of Chuck's hand as he lay there on the ground. He stood up she went to kick him but before she could he grabbed her leg, pulling her and landing on her back. He started moving towards her. She immediately jumped up to her feet and started punching and kicking Chuck in multiple locations. He tried to block but she was too fast.

Mira punched the first twin three times in the face until she grabbed Mira's arm and twisted it back. She reached down and placed her hand between Mira's thighs grabbing her crotch through her jeans, groping Mira a little. She was enjoying this to say the least. That was more then could be said for Mira. The twin placed the other hand under Mira's arm, picking her up, and body slamming her down. Mira laid there motionless and dazed. Blood and dirt marked the right side of her face. The twin sat down on a ventilation shaft next to her and picked her up with ease. A smile grew on her face as she laid her across her knees and slowly began rubbing Mira's small butt.

"You have been a bad girl, Mira." She said somehow knowing her name. She leaned down close to Mira's ear whispering softly.

"A very bad girl." She slapped her gently a few times on the butt grabbing a handful of Mira's hair, pulling her head up towards hers. The twin leaned in placing a hand gently on Mira's cheek giving her a passionate kiss, forcing her tongue into Mira's mouth massaging it with Mira's tongue.

The other twin noticed this, and an appalling stare she gave her sexually frustrated counterpart. "Stop fucking around. You know what Axe said." The twin looked at the other, then at Mira, and pushed her off onto the ground. She stood up and walked over to her.

"I guess we should just get this over with." Chuck lay motionless the same as Jack. The twin made her way towards Mira, she looked at her with great resentfulness.

"What's the matter, Mira? You know you can't do anything to me." Mira swiftly stood up.

"Watch me, bitch." Mira kicked her in the knees, she fell forward, sliding over a ledge grabbing hold of Mira's arm holding on with every ounce of strength. The other twin started to run towards her, but was stopped by Chuck holding onto her ankle. He had regained consciousness.

"Don't let me fall, Mira." Mira tried to pull the twin back up as she reached out her other hand for her. The twin grabbed Mira's hair pulling her down. They both went over. Mira tried to grab something but only grabbed the camera taking it with her. They fell four stories. Below, was a huge stone statue of a strong man holding a barrel under one arm and making a fist towards the sky with the other. Mira held the twin under her as they fell, her eyes bugging with fear. They plummeted. The twin landed on the statue, snapping her spine like a twig. Mira landed on top of her.

*   *   *   *

Fire Rain
4:20 PM

*   *   *   *

The flames were a huge mass of untamed destruction engulfing everything in its path. Even with the continuous fall of rain upon the blaze it continued to roar growing ever larger. The cross perched high atop the steeple burned like a Mississippi Klan's member had placed it in front of the home of an African American family in the 1960's. The hundreds of souls inside now silenced. Pieces of blazing wood and timber fell to the ground. The final judgment had been passed on those, only god knows if they left this earth clean of there sins in the final hour.

I bowed my head saying a small prayer for them, standing there one leg up on a stone garden surrounding a tree. Slowly I peeled the sleeve bandage away from the wound Axe had put in my leg. It was purple and black but not nearly as big as I thought, still deep and painful. The bleeding had stopped though, at least that was something. It was my first official stab wound in the line of duty. I have been shot twice, and now stabbed once.

I looked at my watch 4:20 PM, four hours had passed since the explosion. No sign of reinforcements, no contact with the outside due to the loss of my radio. I thought about the man who called himself The Axe, I was reminded of him every time I looked at the stab wound in my thigh.

I thought about how he claimed that I was some how supposed to have a clue what it was they wanted. What a crock of shit, I didn't know, I didn't care either. The only thing I cared about was taking them down and saving as many innocent lives as possible. Still one thing continues to play over, and over in my head that he said. It was about the dark curtain of deceit, and lies. I could not place my finger on it but I knew, somehow I knew I heard that before. I rubbed between my eyes trying to remember, it was aggravating me.

Suddenly becoming dizzy and ill, my head throbbed and I felt faint. I lost my balance and fell down on my back. The world spun around me in circles, then there was blackness.

When I awoke, I found the Commissioner standing over me, face completely masked by a cloud off smoke. The rain had stopped and a beautiful rainbow arched over the island. The fire was out as well. How long was I out? I thought. Maybe it was all over now.

The Commissioner out stretched his hand to lift me to my feet, I reluctantly accepted. I sat down on the stone garden around the tree. My head still throbbed, I reached into my jacket pocket.

"Where's my Tylenol?" I asked out loud, I pulled out a bottle of Aspirin.

"What the...Aspirin?" Whatever, I thought. I popped four pills, two more then the recommended dosage. The Commissioner puffed away at his cigar.

"How you feeling John?" I rubbed my eyes.

"Confused." He laughed.

"Well, it's normal to be confused, after all I have been training you for a long time now and never once did I tell you what your real mission was." He reached into his jacket pulling out a pack of reds.

"Cigarette?" I pulled a cig out of the pack. He lit it for me.

"Thanks. Now maybe you can tell me what the fuck happened." I took a puff from the cig and began coughing. I don't smoke I thought. What the fuck was I doing? I put the cigarette out on the cement.

"It was Block John. He was behind it all. Him and his cronies of the Cheng Sun Clan."

"The Cheng Sun clan?"

"They disguised themselves in black trench coats. The trench coats were devised of full body armor making it hard for us to take them down. There sunglasses were body armor as well."

"How the freak did they see?"

"Who knows. They had a tactical diversion for taking over the city. A virtual army of minions in black trench coats. Total cataclysmic chaos, but we exposed them."

"How did you stop them?"

"We didn't."

"What do you mean? There still out there?"

"There everywhere, John. You know that."

"You lost me. How do I know that? The only thing I know is these guys took over the island and Wes Adams has something to do with it."

He took a puff of his cigar reaching in his pocket for the pack of smokes.

"Need another cigarette?" I took the cigarette and again he lit it for me. Taking in a drag, I coughed.

"What the freak?" I looked at the cigarette, and put it out where the other was.

"I cant believe you have not figured it out John, all this training, and for what? So you could become a mindless drone?" I stopped him.

"What did you say?" He took another puff.

"So you cold become a mindless drone." I remembered what the Axe called me.

"Where's Mira, Chuck, and Jackie?" He blew out a huge cloud of smoke almost surreal, nearly impossible for the human lung to handle. It seemed to make distorted surreal faces of skulls in clusters, almost cartoon like.

"There are those among us who live on one side of the dark curtain, and there are those on the other. Choose wisely, or betrayal is most certain." I rose to my feet. Something was wrong. Everything seemed out of place.

"Who are you?" He stood up slowly taking the cloud of smoke with him.

"What's the matter John? Feeling confused again?" I looked around there was no one but us.

"Why don't you take some more Aspirin." I reached into my pocket, It was Tylenol this time, as if I imagined the Aspirin from before.

"Sometimes all we need is something to remind us, and we can return to reality. Tell me do you have the time?" I looked at my watch.

"Its 4:20." I remember checking the time just before I passed out it was 4:20 then, impossible, not even a minute has passed? He laughed.

"Thank you, John." I opened my eyes to find everything back the way it was; the fire was still a blaze, the rain poured down on my face as I lay there, the Commissioner was gone, I was dreaming.

I rose to my feet and made my way towards the green plant house next to the blaze. Inside was a vast array of plant life and fountains. There was a wood bridge that led over a lower level of the greenhouse. I crossed it looking to the left and right for any signs of someone. On the other side of the bridge a dead security guard lay in the path. I leaned down close to him. His badge read Henry J. Walt. I had no idea who he was. But as long as he was willing to contribute somehow I didn't care. And ah, yes a flashlight and desert eagle forty five lay next to him. Thanks Henry J. Walt.

The rain made a gentle tapping on the glass high above. The greenhouse was rather hot compared to the outside. I wiped the sweat from my brow. I was surrounded by tall trees and bushes that created a puzzling living maze. If I only knew more about this island. Then maybe I could navigate it with ease. Instead of constantly fumbling around in the dark.

Out of the darkness a flashlight beamed down on me. I looked up to see a shadowy figure holding a flashlight down on me from atop the greenhouse. There was a section of glass missing.

"Who goes there?" Cried a familiar mans voice.

"Officer John Paddock." I cried out.

"No way. Is that you man?" I held my hand over my eyes attempting to see who exactly I was talking to.

"Yeah its me…is that you Chucky?" I stepped back a little trying to get out of the light. But it followed me.

"How do I know it's you?" I asked taking a quick peek behind me just to be sure we were alone.

"I swear to God if you accidentally drop any of that fucking chew out of your mouth on me, I'll kick your ass." Chucky laughed loudly.

"Alright, it's you." He turned the flashlight off.

"Where's Mira and Jack?"

"We ran into some trouble with these twin bitches. We all got separated. I had one of them on the run and then I lost her and found you. What are you doing down there anyway?"

"Trying to find you guys. Twin bitches?"

"Yeah, fucking twins. They kicked are asses, Mira and one of them…"

"What? What happened?"

"Nothing man. Forget it."

"Is she alright?"

"I don't know, she fell and..."

My heart dropped, Mira couldn't be dead. Suddenly there was a crash of shattering glass from behind. The room was becoming engulfed by the flames from outside. Trees were a blaze. The area was filling up with smoke and flames quickly.

"Chucky, I don't know my way out of here. If you can see, your going to have to guide me out." He gave a nod.

"Alright follow me man." He started moving above me through the maze with a birds eye view. It became harder and harder to keep up with him. I had to not only make way through the labyrinth, but also look up to follow him.

I looked up and he was gone. I quickly raced around back tracking, going from right to left, but to no avail I had lost him. The flames were growing closer. I looked down one path it was engulfed in flames. The other also engulfed. Behind me the fire moved in. Then the glass above me shattered from a shot gun blast. I covered my head as the sharp shards came raining down on me. A rope dropped down beside me.

"Sorry about that, man. I found a spot to tie this rope around. There's no way your gonna get out any other way. I looked."

"Okay," I said.

I remembered my military training on how to shimmy up a rope. Of course, I have not had to use it since basic, but we'll see how this goes.

"I'm coming up." I started to make my way up the thick rope. It was easily more then a one hundred foot climb to the top.

"How we doing up there Chuck?" There was no response.

"Hey, Chucky man. How we doing?" Still nothing. I paused for a moment about half way up the rope. Looking up I could see nothing but darkness. There was a flash of lightning that revealed two figures. Then out of the sky came falling my lifeless long time friend and teammate, His throat had been slashed open. He fell just passed me down into the flames below.

"Chucky!" I cried out as I watched him become cremated before my very eyes. I looked up to find one of the twins Chuck was talking about. She was bending over the side looking down on me smiling with the knife that had taken my friend's life in hand. His blood still dripping from the blade.

She started to cut the rope, I quickly made my way up climbing faster then I ever thought possible. But it was to late. Almost to the top, the rope snapped and I was plummeting more then one hundred feet to the fire below. Everything was flashing through my mind, but the one thing that stuck out was avenging my friend's death. I thought if Chuck died and I was going to die, then we all would die.

I removed the forty five from my holster, gripping it in both hands I aimed straight up at her. I pulled the trigger. The bullet seemed to race upward in slow motion. For a moment, it felt as though I was suspended in midair, watching and waiting for that bullet to make contact. Then at least I could die knowing I avenged my friend.

The bullet crashed through the glass shattering it into a thousand shards and then striking its final target. It shot through her stomach, making an exit out the other side. Leaving behind a huge gapping hole. She wore a look of shock on her face as if she was thinking this is not possible. She fell down into the flames of hell along with me.

CHAPTER 12

▼

Their All Dead
6:15 PM

He sat upon his throne. His throne of betrayal. Of carnage. Of hate. Of crates and boxes. He sat upon it one leg propped up on a stool. His head lay rest in his hand. He tapped the arm of his throne with the other. Wes Adams, a man with a long history in the force, was now a monster. Leading an army of terrorists, death and destruction. How he has befouled his own name, the name he worked so hard to make in this city? And what motive did he wish to achieve? What purpose did he have? Who was the one he served, and why? Sitting there waiting. Waiting for the time when all this will end. And whether or not he would achieve his goal.

I sat there for hours trying to understand it all, but still I can not. I have no understanding for why a man with such great intelligence and talent would waste it on this evil. Why would a man who once saved lives, now take them? What drives a man to make such a change?

He walked in to the small storage room in the theater. His hideous face causing me to cringe. The one they called Axe with that smug grin on his disgusting face. Wes Adams frowned lowering his eye brows as he walked in. Axe looked at me and then Wes. He removed his hat to reveal a heavily scarred bald head, huge indents and chunks of skull were missing causing the skin to sink.

"Only a few of us left in the theater, you, me and Axe. That's all. The rest are dead. Thousands of innocent bystanders dead." Wes said to me with sympathy in his voice. Axe opened his jacket looking at a large gapping wound in his side that was untreated, with no bandage of any sort.

"My job was simple, to eliminate the mindless drone and his team. I have accomplished my mission. You have failed yours, Wes." Wes readjusted himself on his throne.

"Failed? No I have completed my mission. But at what cost? I was put in charge of this operation for a reason. Block chose me. Now I fear he has abandoned us." Axe circled slowly around Wes.

"We are expendable, Wes. You knew what was going to happen all along. This was a suicide mission. The odds of us making it off this island alive are minuscule." He leaned in close to Wes and whispered.

"We don't fight for Block. We fight for the purpose." He placed his hat back on. Wes stared into nothingness.

"And where we fail others will triumph. That is how it has always been and so it shall remain." Wes leaned forward.

"Thousands died today. To maintain a secret?" Wes paused and continued. "I don't see the rationalization in that, I don't understand how you can be so callous?" Axe pulled out a shiny hatchet and cloth from his jacket and began polishing it.

"I don't expect an injudicious person such as yourself to understand. This is a secret that has existed for a long time. This was not the first mission of its kind and I caution it wont be the last. Why do you think the American people have remained so tranquil in their little lives all these years?" Wes waved his hand dismissing the question.

"Please Axe, I have heard this speech before. It gives me a headache every time." Axe turned around swiftly with the axe next to Wes's head nearly chopping it off. He had the hatchet resting on his neck before Wes could act.

"Maybe you need to be reminded." Wes pushed him away.

"After all, Wes it was you who said, Hmmm...let me think. Yes I recall now, you said that we fight for a greater tomorrow, to bring this country out of its crime infested immoral cesspool." Axe chuckled a little.

"I did not chose to become a Black Coat. I was given no choice. I love my family and I could never do that to them. Something a man like you would not understand." Axe breathed onto his hatchet and wiped it with his sleeve.

"So you sacrificed the lives of many. For what? To spare the few? How interesting." Wes suddenly became enraged. He spun around and wrapped his hand around Axe's neck nearly picking him up off the ground. He was choking him. But still Axe seemed unaffected. Axe started to laugh a sinister laugh. Wes released him from his grip.

"Once Block arrives I don't ever want to see your ugly face again." Axe looked down at the hatchet.

"If Block arrives." He said under his breath barely audible as he continued to shine the hatchet. It was a remark that puzzled me. What if there is no ending to all this? What if were just waiting until time has expired and then we simply fade away.

✳   ✳   ✳   ✳

??:?? PM
Drowning in a
Sea of Lies

✳   ✳   ✳   ✳

I open my eyes. I see the blur of water above. She stands there looking down upon me. An angel had come to take me to my new home? No, she must be a devil of sorts, come to punish me for my sins. Her arm slowly, gently enters the liquid barrier between us. Her hand open slowly. Her fingers separate into a web. I lay there still. The water waves back and forth masking her face. Who is she? Am I dead? Gently, she cradles me under her arm, lifting me from my watery grave. It was her, the one I loved but never told. She came for me, Mira.

I was free from the waters that saved me. I looked around only to find her looking upon me, the most beautiful smile I had ever bared witness to. She found me. I had fallen to the lower level of the burning building and into a pool with a fountain in the center. I was alive, as was she.

"Mira I'm sorry…I have to tell you…" I said to her without hesitation. She embraced me in her arms not saying a word, merely shaking her head. "Mira, I love you." She placed her hands upon my face. Gently with great passion, she kissed me. It was something I had desired for a long time. When our lips separated, she smiled and I was joyful. Slowly with great grace and a smile on her face, she reached behind her back pulling out one of her nine millimeters. She pressed it slowly to my forehead still beautifully smiling. What was she doing? Maybe this was punishment. As she slowly pulled the trigger, I looked upon her beautiful smiling face one last time. I felt her final embrace. I said goodbye to my angel of death.

✳   ✳   ✳   ✳

4:52 PM
A Sea of Lies
To Drown In

∗   ∗   ∗   ∗

I open my eyes. I see the blur of water above. This time she is not there to greet me. I am alone. It was a dream. A nightmare. My angel has not come, just as well, I'm not ready for her now. Maybe I'll never be. I raised myself out of the water. I was in the pool below the greenhouse. The fire still raged above. Climbing out of the pool, I glanced the room over. It was a small circle at the end of a long hall. There were concession stands and other amenities around. Next to where I sat a store marquee read, -**Lilly's Angel Fire Jewelry Store**-.

I find it harder and harder to separate the facts from reality. I was becoming bewildered. I wiped my face down with a splash of water, even though it was still wet. I looked up to the long fall I had survived. The twin and Chucky were nowhere to be found. Only myself had survived. I knew it would have been impossible for Chuck to have survived, due to the fact that he had a slit throat and the girl had a bullet hole the size of a golf ball in her stomach. Once more fate has intervened.

I stumbled my way down the dark hall still dazed from the fall. How much time had passed since I fell? My watched stopped. It could not have been long or else I would have drowned. I had to find Mira and Jack. I had to find Wes Adams. I tried my radio again. It now had water damage, on top of being half destroyed. It was no use. I whipped it at the wall, shattering it into a hundred pieces.

As I stumbled through the hall I pulled my gun out and reloaded. My head throbbed. I reached in my pocket for my bottle of Tylenol. Shaking it out only a single pill fell into my hand. Damn it, I thought. I needed more than one. Glancing around the hall, I found a nearby pharmacy.

"These guys thought of everything when the built this place." I said to myself.

Inside the pharmacy was filled with miscellaneous items, from shampoo to cigarettes. I grabbed a bottle off the shelf. The thought crossed my mind to grab a pack of smokes after that dream I had earlier. I immediately shook my head dismissing it. No way was I taking up smoking again, not even at time like this. I saw a can of chew, Chuck's brand. I stopped and stared at it for a moment. As I looked at the chew, I opened the bottle of Tylenol popping five more pills dwelling on the can of chew. I had to do it. I owed him that much at least. I snatched the chew off the shelf and made my way out back towards the fountain.

I found it easier to walk this time. Maybe I was more coherent now. I stood there looking down at my reflection in the water. I stood there chew in one hand, gun in the other. The blaze still roared above. I only hoped the floors were made of concrete and would not start collapsing around me.

"This is for you friend." I pulled a handful of chew out, sprinkling it slowly into the water. It fell from my hand like fresh cut grass in the summertime blowing in the wind. I stood there motionless for a time, staring at the floating shreds of chew on the water. I tried as hard as I could to remember the times when Chuck was alive. He has only been gone but a moment, but still I find them slipping away. It was horrifying. I did not want to forget. "Never forget." They took Bobby and now Chuck. This ends now.

I made my way swiftly down the halls. I didn't know where I was going and I didn't care. Rage and hate filled my heart to the brim. I would kill every last one, including and especially Wes Adams. He told me once never trust your best friend with your wife, because he will be the first to fuck you by fucking her. Not your worst enemy. At first I took it in a literal sense, now I think about all the things Wes had said to me. Almost everything had a hidden meaning, such as what he said to me just moments before the blast, better get inside. There's a storm coming. He said it then and I never stopped to think about it.

I passed another corridor and the lights only flickered down it. There was mostly darkness. Something inside told me to stop, turn around, and check out the corridor. Hearing a noise I drew my gun clutching it in both hands, creeping up, sliding with my back to the wall. My heart pounded, my pulse raced, I slowly peaked around the corner, and there was no one. Slowly I crept around the corner sliding across the wall. I came to a window from a store. I stopped, not wishing to cross the window till I knew what was behind it. I stood there counting down one, two, three...I swung around the corner my gun ready. My heart dropped as the face of a mutilated zombie was looking at me. Blood oozed from its sunken eyes. It was frightful and disturbing. It was merely a mask from a novelty shop.

I let down my guard taking in a deep breath. I was clutching my chest and breathing heavy. Then I heard the sound again. It was the distinct sound of a sobbing. Following the sound, I came to a small corridor that led to bathrooms. A man lay dead with a bullet to the chest. A young boy no older then five years lay out over his stomach sobbing. He was embracing the dead man in his arms. I crouched down on one knee. The boy looked up at me and jumped back with a fright. "Don't worry, I'm not going to hurt you." The boy hid under a drinking water fountain.

"Its okay. What's your name?" He said nothing. I looked down at the dead man.

"My name is John. I'm a police officer. I'm here to help you. Please, don't be afraid." I pulled out my badge.

"Look, see this is my badge. Only police have these. I wont hurt you." His eyes welled up in tears.

"I'm sorry." I looked at him puzzled.

"Sorry for what?" He wiped a tear from his cheek.

"I didn't mean to." I scooted up closer placing a hand on his shoulder.

"Didn't mean to what?" He pulled his knees up to his chin wrapping his arms around them.

"To go to the bathroom." Go to the bathroom? What in God's name was he referring to? I looked at the bathroom door, then peaked around just to make sure no one was there.

"What happened when you went to the bathroom?"

"My daddy died."

"How did he die?"

"I don't know. We escaped from the bad men, and I asked my daddy if I could go to the bathroom. He said he was gonna wait outside in case the bad men came." He sniffled.

"And then I heard a loud noise. And I got scared and hid inside the stall. I put my legs up on the toilet so the bad men couldn't find me."

"Did the bad men come in the bathroom?" He nodded.

"And they didn't find you huh?" He shook his head.

"I miss my daddy. I should have held it till we got home." I was never more sadden in my life, to hear this little boy cry and blame himself for his father's death.

"Its not your fault…I'm sure your daddy would have done anything for you." Tears began welling up in my own eyes.

"Hey, do you have a mommy?" He nodded in reply.

"Well I bet she really misses you. We should get you home cause she's probably worried sick." He wiped his nose with his fingers.

"I don't want to leave my daddy." That was it. The tear jerker. I couldn't stop it. Tears slowly ran out from my eyes. I rubbed them attempting to maintain professionalism. I looked at the boy and his father.

"Did your daddy have anything he really liked. Like a watch or something?" He leaned over pointing at his father's wrist watch.

"He liked his watch that me and mommy got him on fathers day." I pulled the stretch band silver watch off his wrist.

"Here. Every time your sad or lonely, just look at this watch you gave your daddy and remember he will always be there watching you. Even if you can't see him." He took the watch.

"Now come on." I out stretched my hand. "Lets take you home to see mommy." He took my hand and stood.

"Wait. I have to say good bye." He knelt down and hugged him.

"I love you daddy." Another tear rolled down my cheek. I let out a deep breath looking to the sky. The boy came up along side me taking my hand.

"Come on, lets go." I picked him up placing him on my hip. We walked away and then I understood. I understood what Mira meant about her biggest fear being death and leaving her daughter alone. I understood.

We walked the corridors. The boy still resting on my hip, playing with his father's watch. He was dressed in a Cubs uniform, hat and all. I was never big on baseball, football was more my game. I rubbed my chin feeling the patch that Axe's hatchet had sliced off my two day old goatee.

"So you like the Cubs?" He looked at me and smiled.

"Yeah, they played pretty good this year huh?" I asked.

"Not really." He said with a simple shrug, tapping his temple as if he were lost in thought.

"They always mess up when they get close to the world series." I chuckled a little.

"Well there's always next year." Yeah right I thought, not in my lifetime.

"My Daddy and me would play catch on Saturdays, but today he decided to take me to the island." I was speechless. This kid kept blaming himself. A five year old boy with a guilty conscience. When I was five, I could have put the cat in the microwave and not given a shit.

"Do you ever play catch with your daddy Mr. Police man?" He asked. I thought of my father, he passed away last summer of cancer. He smoked till the day he died. It was the motivating force I needed to quit myself.

"I used to, but I don't see him any more." He looked at me with puzzlement.

"Why not?"

"My daddy…well he…moved real far away."

"Do you miss him?"

"Very much…but I will see him again someday. Just like you will see your daddy again."

"When I go up to heaven, right?"

"Yeah."

"Oh my God, John!" It was Mira running towards me with Jackie.

"Mira!" I put the boy down. She wrapped her arms around me. It was the first sign of affection she had ever shown me on duty.

"I understand now." Whether or not she understood what I meant, I didn't matter. All I needed was the smile and she gave it to me. She smiled that smile I had truly missed. Jackie extended his hand and I shook it firmly the way we did Kuwait.

"Its good to have you back old friend." Mira looked down at the boy who was shying behind my leg.

"Who's this John?" I placed my hand on his head.

"This is...hey, what is your name?" He looked at Mira completely bashful.

"Its Doc." Mira and I exchanged glances.

"Doc? That's interesting. Is that your real name?" He shook his head.

"No, its just the name my daddy calls me." Mira out stretched her hand.

"Well, it's a pleasure to meet you, Doc." He shied away again behind my legs.

"John, Jackie and I have made some interesting discoveries since you have been gone like the trench coats they wear for one..." I interrupted her.

"Sorry to interrupt Mira but...Chucks...He's no longer with us." Her jaw dropped. She turned her body hiding the tears. Jack took in a deep breath.

"I just saw him not that long ago on the roof." I rubbed two hands together uncomfortably.

"One of the female ones got him. She tried to kill me but I was to fast for her." She nodded wiping a tear away.

"There will be a time to sob later." She said as if to impress me. I placed my hands on her shoulders.

"Are you alright with this? Do you need a few minutes?" She shook her head.

"No, I'm fine John. Anyway, time to change the subject. In addition to discovering the secret of their trench coats. We also uncovered the location of where they are keeping the hostages." She grinned a little through her sorrowed face.

"They have them in the theater. If we move now we can get there before they leave." I raised an eyebrow to her.

"Leave? Where are they going?" Jackie looked at her puzzled as well.

"Yeah, how do you know there going anyway?" Jackie asked. She looked back and forth at Jackie and I.

"Because it makes sense. I mean come on guys, they would not have taken hostages if they had no strategy to get off this island." Jackie pulled out the Spas he had received from Chucky.

"I'm cocked and ready to kick ass!" I looked down at Doc.

"Well, what about him? I mean we can't take him with us and we can't just leave him here." We all exchanged glances. Jack rubbed his stomach as if he were starving, which he probably was.

"Well, don't look at me. I am not playing babysitter." Jack looked around. He seemed focused on a fast food joint.

"Wait, what about Jerome?" I looked at her puzzled.

"Who's Jerome?" I asked. She looked behind the way they had come.

"Jerome is a security guard hiding out in a supply room back that way." Jack stopped his focus on the fast food.

"Yeah, she's right. We found him there a little ways back." I picked Doc up, placing him on my hip.

"Let's go!"

✱   ✱   ✱   ✱

The Hideaway

✱   ✱   ✱   ✱

"Jerome!"

"Who goes there?"

"Its me Mira."

"What do you want? I thought I told you how to get to the theater."

We stood outside the locked room in the hall. It read janitor's office on the door. I talked with a low voice to Jack as she tried to get him to open the door.

"How many of these guys would you say is left?" I asked. He shrugged.

"Don't know exactly, I haven't seen one since the roof. My guess is less then ten." Jack said. Mira continued to attempt to get the guard to open up. He seemed a little edgy.

"You want to know something funny though? When I got pushed down that shaft on the roof, before I woke up, I had the craziest dream. We were here, but everything was all out of place." I nodded.

"Yeah, I have been having some crazy ass dreams myself." Finally he opened the door. As we walked in Jack continued.

"Yeah, it was like we were still here on the island, but the commissioner was here and he was trying to tell me something. He asked if I had ever been familiar with subliminal messages." He said as he rubbed his forehead.

"Jerome Meet Doc. Your going to be keeping an eye on him for me." Jerome, A younger African American man dressed in his white Island patrol uniform, wearing a bulletproof vest that looked like Jackie's, looked at me and Doc.

"Alright, whatever. But who's this guy right here?" He gestured to me.

"This is John, he's in charge." He frowned.

"He's in charge? Man I thought you were in charge?" He sat there on a stack of boxes, pointing at Mira.

"Well It doesn't matter anyway. We're in a hurry so just stay cool. This will all be over soon." He shrugged.

"Whatever, just hurry the fuck up, I want to go home, get me some prime ribs." Jackie outstretched his fist to Jerome. They knocked fists in an obscure handshake.

"Fuck yeah man! That's what I'm talking about. I'm fucking starving. Get me some burgers." Jack said as he rubbed his stomach.

"Alright, lets go." I put Doc down. Getting down on one knee I placed my hands on his shoulders.

"Okay Doc, your going to be safe with Jerome here. He's kind of like a police officer, but more rented." Jerome rolled his eyes at me.

"It will be okay. I will come back for you and take you to your mom personally." He nodded and gave me a hug.

"Okay, be good."

＊　　　＊　　　＊　　　＊

Storm and Sun
7:34 PM

＊　　　＊　　　＊　　　＊

We set foot outside, the storm was passing, only a few clouds hovered over head. A few small drops still fell from above. Everything was wet, it made for increasing humidity causing the heat index to rise worse then before. The sun peaked through the clouds. We were in the very center of the island, surrounded by walls of brick. There were no openings and you had to go through the building to get out. It was a vast garden filled with the tallest trees on the island I have seen yet. They looked as if they had been here for centuries. Of course, that was impossible, maybe they flew them in from a forest somewhere. All the pathways led to a stone circle in the middle of the garden. In the center of that was a mix of flowers and a huge statue of man holding a large fish. Kind of ridicules looking really. He had this dumbfounded expression like he was stoned beyond belief. I would like to find the guy who made this ugly thing and kick his ass.

The pathways were cobble stone. They were lined with stone benches and trash bins. There were birds of every sort, perched on the limbs of the trees, all singing their little bird songs about shitting on cars. All glad the storm had passed and they got their little bird shower. There were small speakers hidden under the flower beds. I stopped to listen to one and a song played that came out back when I was in high school. Unfortunately due to expensive copyright law I shall refrain from singing it.

"Jerome said we had to go through the garden into the east corridor." We stood by the circle with the statue.

"Well, that must be the east corridor if the sun is behind us right now." I looked behind up at the sun it was more or less southwest.

"No. That's wrong. Unless your Jerome guy is completely wrong, the east corridor is over there." I pointed towards a bunch of trees and bushes.

"I don't see any door there." I started walking towards it.

We made it to the trees and bushes, but there was no sign of any door. "I don't get it, it should be right here, unless its northeast." She rubbed her head.

"No. He specifically said do not take the northeast corridor. It's a dead end." Jack looked around then hopped up on to the stone wall surrounding the bushes. He made his way through them until he was out of sight.

"I found it!" He called out. Mira and I exchanged glances. "It's over here guys, hidden behind all this growth."

Mira and I walked through the bushes. He was right. On the other side hidden deep in the growth was a doorway.

"Weird, huh?" There was barely enough room for us to fit between the door and the growth.

"Yeah, why would it be back here?" Mira looked at the door. It was steel, not much to look at.

"It must be an emergency exit or something. A back service door maybe. Who knows, maybe they just messed up when they designed it." Mira pushed the metal handle down opening the door.

"Whatever. Who cares, let's go."

Inside was a narrow hall, not even wide enough for two people to walk side by side. It was dark and barely lit at all.

"Are you sure this guy knew what he was talking about?" I asked her as she walked behind me.

"Yes, he said there would be a long narrow hall and then another clearing outside. But this one would be still under construction. A part of the island they were unable to finish in time. It actually will be an addition to the theater. A performance play stage." Jack spoke from the very back.

"Well, then maybe this is just a construction tunnel until they finish it." I looked at the walls around us.

"That would explain the crappy plastering job on this dry wall. Its most likely a temp wall." Mira interrupted.

"Men, you always have to talk about construction, What is that? When a guy is driving down the road and sees a construction site, he has to gawk at it and ask, I wonder what there building there?" Mira made an interesting point. We do love to check out construction.

"It's a guy thing, Mira, cant explain, just have to except it." She frowned.

"A guy thing huh?"

"Yep."

✳   ✳   ✳   ✳

Bad Timing
7:48 PM

✳   ✳   ✳   ✳

We came out into the unfinished clearing, construction vehicles were scattered everywhere, along with stacks of steel and brick. It was the site of some recent construction, the workers were probably just here yesterday, setting up. Only a few beams were over head, the roof itself was nowhere near completion. The concrete had been laid, but only enough to support the weight of the massive island.

"Now where Mira?" She looked around the large area, her hand being used as a visor to block the sun.

"Over there." She pointed to another metal service door on the other side. We started walking to it. Suddenly, a chopper flew in above, it looked the same as ours.

"Damn it! Now they send in reinforcements."

Five men dressed the same as us, only with gas masks on, dropped down behind a dump truck. One was inside the cab of the truck itself. Two of them went running around to the other side of a crane.

"I don't like the looks of this." Mira said to me. I had to agree, something was not right about these guys.

"Take cover!" They opened fire on us. Why would they open fire on us? We're the good guys. This had to be some sort of misunderstanding. Mira ducked and rolled under a truck. Jack and I jumped behind a stack of steel beams.

"Fuck! I'm hit." Jack said as he lay there on the ground clutching his chest.

"Why aren't you wearing your vest man?!" I pressed my hand on his chest attempting to slow the blood.

"I had to take it off. I gave it to Jerome to help him calm down a bit." Blood was drenching his "Have a nice day mother fucker" smiley face T-shirt.

"Your bleeding pretty bad." He winced in pain.

"Yeah, I guess I am." He looked at me with great pain in his eyes.

"John, you and I both know what to do when a soldier has fallen and there's no chance of survival." My hands were covered in his blood. I knew what he meant, it was a code we had followed since the war.

"No man, your gonna make it." He shook his head slowly expressionless.

"No…I'm not. I took a bullet to the chest, one of their bullets…don't let me die by the enemies hand. I don't want to die slowly. Give me my dignity." He coughed up blood, I shut my eyes tightly, pressing my lips together. Slowly I placed my gun to his forehead. My hand shook, my lips quivered.

"I'm sorry bro, I'm sorry." I did not open my eyes not wishing to look at his face.

"Its alright, I'll see you on the other side. Your ass better be good fucker, cause I know I'm going to heaven." I nodded slowly.

"I wont forget."

"You better not."

Never forget the fallen ones. A code that the three of us had wrote into the book as of today, the unfinished book of the prototype special forces unit. I tried my hardest to block out all sound around me, to put myself in another place, I kept my eyes shut tight as I pulled the trigger. As my best friends blood sprayed my face I turned around not wishing to see him as I slowly open my eyes. I wiped the blood off my face with my hand. The gun I held with great rage, this gun will forever be my weapon of vengeance. The gun I retrieved off a fallen security guard, another name on the list of the fallen.

I peaked around the corner. One of the men was sitting in the operation cab of the crane. The crane started moving. He swung the hook and ball straight through the window of the truck Mira hid under shattering the glass. The hook lodged itself into the roof of the truck like a hook on a fish, but this fish was a big Dodge Ram all wheel drive extended cab with a Hemi. The truck slowly lifted off the ground, Mira crawled out from under it. The truck leaned to one side because the hook was not centered. Mira jumped into the tilted extended bed of the truck. It was riddled with bolts and nails that made clanking sounds as they shifted from one side to the other. I thought to myself, what the fuck was she doing? Was she crazy?

I moved around the other side to the three men behind the dump truck. I came up to an opening between a stack of bricks, and a stack of beams. As I jumped through the opening, one of them peaked over the top of the dump truck, flying through the air like a quarterback sneak going for the touchdown. I outstretched my arm firing at him, hitting him dead in the neck.

The chopper still hovered above, I wondered if they had guns up there and would open fire at any given time. Mira was lifted high above with the truck about one hundred feet. He swung her towards a wall, just before she hit. She jumped off into a dive formation both guns drawn hand and hand. The truck was destroyed by the impact. Mira fired four shots straight down as she fell, the man in the crane fell out dead. She aimed one arm to the right, and the other to the left firing off six rounds at the other two simultaneously, nearly taking them out at the same time. Her descend came to an end in a large vat filled with unmixed cement powder. Only one left, only one masked man, only one out of five who flew in from the sky, taking my best friends life. Nothing mattered, nothing but revenge.

"You got one last chance. One shot. One opportunity to give up…" I cried out from behind the stack of steel beams that masked me.

"I know what your thinking, why should I trust this guy? He just killed all my buddies. Why wouldn't he do the same to me twice as fast? Well I'll tell you right now, I'm an officer of the law and my word is as good as my friendship." I peaked around the corner, there was no sign of him. Mira was crawling slowly out of the vat, she was covered head to toe in powdered cement. Just add water I thought. Fortunately, for her it was no longer raining.

"I'm giving you on last chance to come out with your hands up, If not…Well, we can always come in guns blazing." There was a long pause until he finally emerged from behind the dump truck, hands clasped behind his head.

I slowly walked towards him with my gun in both hands aimed and ready. Mira came up along side of him in a similar stance. I walked up to him, my gun no more then a foot from his neck, my finger danced on the trigger. Mira stood to the side of him gun aimed straight for his head.

"Don't you fucking move!" He stood there motionless. My reflection was in his gas mask, I could see the monster this place was making me. My thirst for vengeance needed to be quenched.

"Remember you said you wouldn't kill me." He said with an uneasy tone. My heart beat faster and faster, rage pumped through my veins.

"Yeah, I know what I said. I said my word is as good as my friendship, but since you put a bullet in my best friend's chest, I guess my word is no good." I pulled the trigger, blowing a hole straight through his neck, he fell directly backwards.

I slowly lowered my gun. Mira just stood there. I could tell what she was thinking, John just shot an unarmed man, she said nothing. Maybe she wanted me to kill him, vengeance was ugly.

"John, I underestimated you." A raspy voice came from the man's radio. Mira and I exchanged glances. I picked it up.

"Who is this?" A man's voice came over, it sounded like someone I knew all to well.

"It's Mr. Cuban." I knew I recognized that raspy voice.

"The Commissioner? Where are you?" He puffed on his cigar as he spoke.

"Look up." Mira and I both looked up at the chopper that hovered above us.

"You have really proven yourself to me that you are ready." These guys were associated with the Commissioner?

"Ready? Ready for what?" There was a long pause, Mira and I exchanged glances. She wore a look of denial as if none of this were true.

"For the war."

I knew his words, but I also knew this was insane. After all these years was he testing me?

"I'm sorry I don't follow, Sir. Exactly what war are you talking about?" The chopper still hovered above, Mira was pacing with intrigue.

"More or less, the unveiling of the nightmare behind our nation. This was a test, it has always been a test. For the past two years, about the same amount of time I had been training you and your team. I was training your replacements." A feeling of anger came over me, I interrupted him.

"Our replacements!?" He took another puff before he continued.

"Yes, John. They were to replace you had you failed your mission. They were ready if you expired, but I decided to have them kill you instead." He paused taking in another drag.

"You know the rules. Your expendable, you were getting sloppy, letting your team die around you." His cold hearted words were enraging me. This was a man I had trusted with my life. Betrayal seemed to follow me this day, like a hunter with its prey.

"What the fuck is going on? How did you know about Chuck and Bobby?" I demanded. I looked at the empty shell of a man I had just ended, it was by my hand he left this earth, and the Commissioner saw everything.

"Shouldn't you be more curious as to why I tried to kill you?" I swallowed with no reply.

"That's interesting..." He said mockingly. "Fine don't reply. As I was saying. I decided to take the initiative to end things now. Unfortunately the replacements were not ready, and you proved to be the best, regardless of your fallen teammates." I was at the edge, I lost it, taking the radio and flinging it at the dump truck shattering it. How can this son of a bitch be so pompous. A man I trusted. A man I respected. Mira looked at me, she was at a loss for words. All this time I never saw it coming. We were set up.

"John, pick up the radio." The Commissioner said. His voice came from another radio held by one of the other dead replacements not far away. I stood there leaning over, my hands resting on my knees. I was breathless, looking over to the other radio, I took in a deep breath and with unsteady hands I picked up the two way.

"Alright." I rubbed my eyes with frustration.

"Good. Those kind of violent temperaments are the reason I was never quite sure if you were ready. I'm sorry John. I had no choice. I know this is kind of sudden, but you should have seen it coming. All the warning signs were there. Why do you think the Mayor and I had been working together all these years?" He asked. I smiled attempting to relieve some pressure.

"I don't know. Maybe I'm fighting for the wrong team, and these guys are doing us a favor." I said sarcastically. The Commissioner sighed.

"No John. There are no such things as teams, only rules. I used you to get to them. Why did you kill that unarmed man? Why John? You know as well as I do that's not police procedure, but you did it anyway. To avenge the death of your friend? We all do things we know are not moral, but there are exceptions. To continue to fight for what we believe in. I believe we are doing what is right." I rolled my eyes.

"Spare me the fucking moral lecture Commissioner. Get to the fucking point."

He puffed away. "You think this was a simple terrorist act? Terrorism is not even in the same ball park, John. Their running the show, not us. What you experienced today, was merely a small taste of the hell they have unleashed on this country for many decades. The Mayor knew, the same as I, that this day would come, the beginning." I walked around the area slowly.

"So you left us out here to die." He took another drag.

"I did what I had to do."

I remembered all he had taught me about Block, and how one day he would lead a band of terrorists to the city.

"What about Block? What's he have to do with all this?"

"Block? Block is nothing more then a pawn in their game. They used him as a cover up, someone to point the finger, as they always have."

"How? What did they do to get him to take the fall?"

"Offered him money, power, maybe they held a gun to his head. Who knows? They use many techniques to recruit their masses."

"I guess I'm just a pawn in the game too."

"We're all pawns in the game, John. The question is who's winning?"

The Mayor, Wes Adams, the Commissioner, and Block. They were all linked.

"So the Mayor knew to much, and they had him eliminated right? That's what this is all about." Mira sat down on a rusty tool chest clasping her hands together as she listened.

"Precisely John. An assassination. The Mayor was going to expose them today in his speech to all the world. Whether or not the world would listen was anybody's guess. Somehow they found out. A leak John. For security purposes, only a select few of us knew about the speech. Their all dead now, all but two, Mr. Johnson the Mayor's esteemed advisor and long time friend, and one other." I paused and thought about Mr. Johnson. Why would he do something like that. I never had the opportunity to meet this man but I have heard much about him. Of course with all the lies and betrayal around, why not? It seems to be the in thing to do.

"Johnson? Who's the other?"

"Think about it long and hard, all the clues are there. The leak could be right under your nose." He paused to puff away at his cigar.

"This conversation has ended." With that remark he took off in his chopper.

One hour ago

"I already explained this to you, it was about an hour before the incident with the Commissioner."

I awoke to find myself laying on top of the twin. She did not survive, her back was shattered from the fall. Which I was grateful for because she broke my fall, but still knocked me out for God knows how long. I was soaked from the rain and a little incoherent. I managed to find a way to shimmy down the arm of the statue to the ground. Even with the bulletproof vest on my chest ached from the impact. I could have used a few of John's Tylenols at that point. I don't know how exactly I survived the fall, but I was alive, and that's all you need know. I knew I had to complete the mission, so I sought out to find John.

I walked that island backtracking to the direction in which I thought he might be. Instead of finding John, I found someone else. I heard his moans from a good distance, and I knew it was him. I thought he was dead, but he survived.

"Jackie!"

"Oh my head." He said as he lay there with his arm tossed over his shoulder in the bushes. He was bruised and battered, but for the most part he was okay.

"Oh man, what happened?" I wrapped my arm around him to help him to his feet.

"I don't know, I think you fell down a ventilation shaft and luckily ended up in theses bushes." He squinted his eyes, making a slight moan of pain as if they were burning.

"All I remember is that bitch beating the shit out of me." He glanced up at the sky.

"And it's fucking raining."

"C'mon, we need to find John."

"Where's Chucky?"

"Still on the roof...I hope."

"Oh...The roof...Why were we on the roof?"

"I'll explain latter."

"Oh good, cause I don't even know where we are right now. What day is it?"

Jack and I made our way through the mall corridors. Jack was showing the signs of battle fatigue. I tried to maintain composure the best I could, after all I was second in command. If John fell, or was not present, Chuck and Jack would take orders from me. John tends to forget how much power I really have. Sometimes I think he belittles me because I am a woman, and he feels I lack the strength. If only he knew. But there was something about him that intrigued me so much. He hid his true self behind this tough guy exterior. I knew his feelings for me, and his jealousy for Bobby. But despite his suspicions, there was nothing going on between Bobby and I. I guess I just felt sorry for him. John was always giving him the most grief. I think more or less Bobby just wanted to fit in. It was tough for him to be transferred here from New York. Imagine a New Yorker cop trying to fit in with a team of Chicago special forces. It does not matter now, but when John was not around Bobby would always tell me how much he truly respected and looked up to John. I tried to convince him to stop acting so hard headed all the time and John would accept him. But Bobby was convinced it was John's prejudice against New Yorkers that kept him from accepting him...And now he's gone.

"Man I am starving." Jack said out of the blue. He had been eyeing restaurants ever since we walked in here. I couldn't even think about food right now. Suddenly he deviated from the path walking into a pastry restaurant.

"Officer Brown! What do you think you're doing?" I demanded. But he seemed to be focused more on the pastry. His mouth seemed to water as he stared at the cinnamon roll under the glass. He tapped the glass as if to catch its attention like a child looking into a fish tank.

"Is it wrong?" He asked.

"Yes. Lets go."

"But it looks so tasty."

"Its illegal. We cant just take anything we want just because there's no one around to stop us."

"But ma'am I think under the circumstances…" I interrupted.

"What circumstances Brown?"

"Forget it." He said to me as if I were his mother. Sometimes I stop and wonder if they all think I treat them like their mother. I follow the rules. Growing up with my uncle Leo taught me this. His only rule was to follow the rules. He said with his Italian accent, someday, Mira you will make a man very happy because you followed the rules. I wonder if uncle Leo really knew.

"What do you think about John?" I asked Jack catching him off guard.

"As a person or an officer?"

"A person."

"Well I've been friends with him forever, and uh personally, I think he's one of the greatest guys I've ever known."

"Okay how about as an officer?"

"He leads his team like we were his children in a way. Always molding us, making us stronger, smarter, everyday."

"So you consider him to be a father figure?"

"That's not what I meant. I mean it's just the way he leads. I don't think of him as a father, I think of him as a friend."

"Do I come off as being too much like a mother?"

"What do you mean?"

"Never mind."

"No tell me."

"It's not important."

Our uncomfortable conversation was interrupted. A crashing sound of something metal came from inside a nearby storage room. I can't say that I was not in the slightest bit relieved by this. The conversation officer Jack Brown and I had been having was going sour.

I silently pointed for Jack to cover one side of the door while I took the other. My guns rested on my chest pointed straight up which was heaving from the sudden change in atmosphere. We were dead center of a three way junction. All I could see was a long dark hall in front of me. Just off to the side was a winding hall that seemed to disappear and reappear. A big stupid looking sign that read -MANS' GREATEST ACHIEVEMENT HOTDOG STAND- In bold neon black lights was all lit up on the one corner of the junction. It stood out like a sore thumb, and was an eyesore to say the very least. Mans' greatest achievement? If the hotdog was mans' greatest achievement, then mankind is truly doomed.

I gave jack a quick nod as if to imply that we were going in. Jumping directly in front of the door I was ready. My guns were also ready both pointed forward towards the door. I gave jack a quick glance and with that the door was kicked open. "Freeze Chicago P.D.!" A security guard was hunched over cowering with his hands in the air.

"Oh snap, I thought you were the mother fuckers in trench coats." He said trembling with his hands still in the air.

"That's who we thought you were."

"Well, I ain't. The names Jerome, security."

"Nice to meet you Jerome. I'm officer Dontonelli, and this is officer Brown."

"Cops good, the cavalry's arrived."

"Not exactly." His hands were still in the air. Jack moved in behind me. The storage room was small and littered with mops and brooms.

"Alright so who are you?" He asked.

"No time to explain, are you alone?" I replied.

"Yeah." He slowly lowered his hands.

"What's going on out there?"

"No time to explain that either. Just stay calm."

"I was calm until you showed up." He paused and looked over my shoulder. "Look out!"

I spun around, a Black Coat was coming this way. Jack unloaded on him. Bullets flew, and then he flew straight back into the "Greatest achievement" hotdog stand. There was a metal bowing sound, and then the neon hotdog sign came loose, crashing down onto the Black Coat. Sparks flew in all directions, and that was the end to "Mans' greatest achievement."

"Man I think I just shit myself." Jerome said slowly shaking his head. Jack looked at me.

"Faulty craftsmanship." Jack simply said.

"Alright. Jerome can you tell me how to get to the theater?" I said.

"Yeah, why do you want to go there?" Jerome asked.

"That's where there keeping the hostages." Jack seemed a bit puzzled by what I just said.

"How'd you know that?" Jack asked me. He looked at me with one brow raised in curiosity.

"Call it a hunch." That was all I could reply. I had no other way to explain it. It was just a hunch and I left it at that.

"Yeah, sure, I know where it's at. I'll give you directions." He said as if this were some off road excursion. Off road maybe, but no way would this be a pleasure trip.

*   *   *   *

Jerome proceeded on to explain how to find the theater. Jack still gave me that look of doubtfulness as to how I knew about the theater. Jack was never the type to ask to many questions, he just did as he was told. He was a very Yes Man. Whatever he had to do, he just did it. In a way I respected that, in another way I knew that would eventually get him killed.

"Thank you, Jerome."

"No problem…hey don't forget to take the east corridor, not the northeast. It's a dead end." I nodded in reply.

"Now your just gonna leave me here to die, huh?"

"Don't worry you will be fine. Just stay in here and wait till the real cavalry arrives." He scratched his head as he slowly nodded. Jack started to remove his bulletproof vest revealing his "Have a nice day mother fucker." T-shirt.

"Here man take this. It might make you feel safer." Jack handed the bullet-proof vest to Jerome.

"What are you doing officer?" I demanded of Jack.

"Don't worry, Mira. I can handle myself without it." It was the one time he didn't listen. So maybe I was wrong, and the time he does not listen is when he would get himself killed.

"You better officer." He simply smiled.

We continued our way through the mall. I couldn't stop thinking about the way Jack looked at me when I mentioned the theater. It was a thought that would continue to drive me insane. I had to tell him, but I couldn't, no absolutely out of the question. He would have to find out later for himself. I only hoped I would not be around when he did. I could not bare to look into his eyes at that moment. Especially John's eyes.

Speaking of. John was coming down the hall in front of us, holding a small child in one arm, and his gun in the other, not exactly the most heartwarming picture I've ever seen. Still my heart filled with joy to see him again. I don't know why I felt this way, it was unexplainable. It remained a feeling I had to continue to suppress if I was to complete my mission. The mission. What was that again? I'd rather not say.

CHAPTER 13

▼

**Fire in the Hole
8:15 PM**

*　　*　　*　　*

"We will not desist, our demands must be met. All we require is a little more time and then the hostages will be free."

*　　*　　*　　*

A movie about a hostage situation played on the big theater screen, highly inappropriate, I thought. How dare they play this at a time like this. Mary sat in my lap, eyes heavy, still unable to sleep. It was only 8:15, yet I myself was exhausted from the days events. I wondered what was going on outside, was anyone even coming for us? Nearly eight hours have passed since the bombing. At least they are providing some entertainment, as inappropriate as it may be.

I thought about eating some warm apple pie, with a side of coffee. My stomach was not happy, nor was my aching back. It had been nearly ten hours since the last time I used the bathroom, a feat I never thought possible, but in a situation such as this, I suppose anything is truly possible. Passing the time which seemed to stand still, was the only thing I could think to do to make a positively dire situation more comfortable. I'm an old man, and even I am exceptionally bored right now. I have overcome the fear that they will kill us now. After seeing the display Mr. Wes Adams put on for us earlier, I know that is not what they want. So now I sit and wait here with my granddaughter. Waiting for the cavalry to arrive and watching this ridiculously bad movie.

✳   ✳   ✳   ✳

Time is Running Out

✳   ✳   ✳   ✳

"I just spoke with the negotiator, again." Wes Adams said pacing in uneven circles, hands clasped behind his back with a look of despair painted on his face. He had been doing this for the past ten minutes or so, it gave me a nervous chill, you know the kind when your sitting down and everyone else is standing around you.

"What did he say?" Axe said, sitting on a cheap plastic chair in the corner, shinning his hatchet again.

"Same thing. We need to let a few hostages go, so they know their alive and well. Oh, and something about the island is on fire." Axe stopped abruptly. His face grew pale, more pale then it already was.

"Fire did you say?" Wes continued to circle.

"Yes, fire. You don't know anything about that do you?" Axe shook his head and continued to shine the hatchet.

"No, not at all. How much of the island is on fire exactly." Wes raised his arms as if to gesture the size.

"I don't know. A good portion of it. He said the church has already burned to the ground, along with the greenhouse, and parts of the shopping center. You remember the church Axe, the one you were in earlier." Wes said with a bit of sarcasm, Axe smiled.

"Yes, I recall. The church with the blasphemies priest. Poor, dear, Brandon Sikes. Terrible way to die." Axe said. Wes stopped and looked at Axe who continued to polish the hatchet.

"What to burn alive?" He asked Axe curiously. Axe frowned not even straying his eyes from the hatchet.

"No the bullet I put through his forehead." He said with a calm serious voice as he breathed onto the hatchet. Wes stopped, and turned to Axe.

"I know you have a bad habit of killing people with that hatchet of yours Axe, but I never thought you to be an arsonist." Axe put the hatchet back in his holster. He crossed one leg over the other, resting his hands on them.

"What could you possibly mean by that? I would never do something so fool hearted like starting the island on fire. Only a criminally insane man with chronic schizophrenia who was horribly scared by his crazed father when he threw boiling hot water at his face would do something like that." Wes took in a deep breath rolling his eyes.

"Whatever, it does not matter now. Block will be here soon, and this will all be over." Axe let out a low chuckle, Wes raised one brow to him.

"What's so funny?" Axe leaned back in the chair.

"Your ignorance amuses me. Continue to speak I find it entertaining." He said with an ugly smile.

"I see…your hideous face amuses me." Axe's grin slowly died.

"Ignorant fool. I'm prepared to die today. You're a pathetic excuse for one of us. I rue the day they recruited you. Block will not be here. If he does, he is more a fool than you." For the first time since I have seen this man called Axe, he speaks with great passion, He truly believes in what he's fighting for, whatever that may be. He slowly rose from his chair never averting his eyes from Wes Adams.

"I'm going to go on check on things." Wes nodded slow and intimidating. Axe left the room. Now I was alone once more with my monster, a man I could not relate, nor talk to, so I will sit here in silence.

*   *   *   *

8:20 PM

*   *   *   *

"This way, John." Mira and I made our way down the hall. We came to some double doors with two windows. I was still thinking about all the Commissioner had said, about the leak and how it could be one of two people. I wondered who the other was.

We ducked down next to the doors. Mira slowly peaked over the top through the window. "I see five, maybe six of them. There's at least a thousand hostages in there. Amazing not one of them has tried to over come these guys." I sat there gun held in both hands.

"Well, sometimes the fear of dying is all it takes to keep someone at bay." Mira slid down the door.

"Human emotion in a crisis situation can be the ultimate weakness." She took in a deep breath. "How do you want to do this Paddock?" I had no idea.

"Well, we can't go in guns blazing because of the hostages, so that rules that out, unfortunately. Are you sure this is the only way in?" She nodded.

"Yeah, Jerome said there were other ways, but this would be the best." She peaked over the top again.

"It looks like there is an access catwalk just to the right of us. If we play our cards right we might be able to locate Adams." I remembered the big ugly oaf that tried to kill me with an axe earlier.

"You don't see a really ugly heavily scarred man anywhere do you?" She shook her head.

"That's good."

Mira and I looked at each other with a simultaneous nod. We opened the door very slowly. We were off in a corner out of sight from the hostages and the Black Coats. All except one little boy with glasses who noticed us. I put my finger to my lips in a shush, he smiled and I returned the gesture.

We crept up the metal stairway to the catwalk. It wrapped around the entire theater. It was long and narrow. Mira walked low behind me, she whispered.

"So what are you going to do after all this is over Paddock?" I thought about how I always wanted to write a book about my life on the force.

"I don't know, maybe write a book, maybe get a movie deal." She laughed a low laugh.

"That's a pleasant thought…incidentally John…there's something I have been meaning to ask you." I thought about the possible things she may want to ask me, there was one in particular that I hoped she was not referring to. I don't know if I could handle that right now.

"Do you think this is an appropriate time to be asking me, Mira?" There was silence and for a moment I thought I had managed to say the wrong thing again.

"I'm sorry Mira, please ask me." She sighed.

"No your right, I'll ask later, I just thought the situation was fitting." What did she mean by the situation? I thought.

*   *   *   *

Mary and Grandfather

*   *   *   *

The movie played on, the main characters found themselves in the middle of a major fire, after they had just struggled to untie themselves from train tracks, Similar to that of an old cartoon, as the two police officers Jenson, and Hodgerson, made there way through the burning building attempting to free the hostages. They were confronted by one of the terrorist that had tied them to the tracks.

"So, you thought you could out smart the great Depressor Mu hahaha!" He said in an irritatingly bad acting voice. The movie was cheesy beyond belief, one of those low budget B movies from the 1980's, with some of the worst acting ever. Suddenly one of the main characters, a young kid about 18 years old with a bad 80's hair cut, removed his mask. "And you thought I was a blond." Just God awful crap.

As the movie played Mary looked up at me still sitting in my lap. "Grandpa, I don't like this movie." She said to me with a frown.

"I know dear, I don't like it either." She rubbed her tummy.

"Grandpa I'm hungry." I knew she had to be just as hungry as I. "Grandpa I have to go to the bathroom." I looked around one of the Black Coats was standing near.

"Excuse me, Sir." He looked at me through those dark sunglasses.

"My granddaughter has to use the rest room. Could I trouble you into escorting us?" He gave me a single nod but no word of reply, Mary and I stood up and followed him down the steep stairway to the bathroom.

"Alright make it quick."

He stood out side the door as I took Mary into the Men's room. It was very clean and fancy, much the same as the rest of the island with high class appeal and down home Chicago charm.

As I stood there waiting for Mary to come out of the stall I glanced down at my hands, they were filthy. As I rubbed soap onto them and rinsed Mary asked, "Grandpa? What's that smell?" She said still in the stall. The air had a slight hint of smoke smell that filled the room. The mirror's reflection revealed an air vent behind me, thick black smoke was oozing from it filling the room. My heart dropped. It was just like the cheap movie playing on the Imax screen, the building was a blaze.

Mary came out of the stall. "Come along Mary we have to hurry!" We made our way swiftly out of the bathroom, The Black Coat was standing outside holding his AK in both hands crossed over his chest.

"We have to get out of here." He gave me a look of confusion.

"Nobody's going anywhere." I shook my head. "No you do not understand, the building is on fire." He glanced around real quick.

"Just return to your seat." I had my face right next to his, with a stern voice I said,

"Now you listen to me, any moment now this entire place is going to go up in a ball of flames, and then your going to really have mass panic, everything is going to be out of control. So I would suggest that you fucking start evacuating!" I was never the type to use profanity's, especially in front of my granddaughter, but in this case I would make an exception. The Black Coat gave me a look of shock, most likely surprised to hear an old man like myself speak to him in such a manor. His attention was abruptly taken away when he started sniffing the air, the aroma of burning wood could be recognized from before.

"What's that smell?"

*   *   *   *

Mira and John

*   *   *   *

We made our way to the bottom of the metal staircase of the catwalk, we were for the most part out of sight, in a long narrow hall. One of the Black Coats stood at the bottom blocking our path. I took the liberty to dispose of him, by coming up from behind and slashing his throat. Mira came up along side me, she was sniffing the air in a most peculiar manner. A faint smell of something burning filled my nostrils. "Do you smell that John?"

*   *   *   *

Wes and Mr. Johnson

*   *   *   *

I sat quietly in the room with Wes Adams, we had not said a word to each other since Axe left. Wes sat there in a daze never moving, then suddenly he seemed startled somehow sniffing the air. He frowned with a look as if he knew exactly what it was, with a simple sigh he cursed. "Fuck."

CHAPTER 14

▼

Panic room
8:37 PM

"We got to get these hostages out now!" The main character Jenson said, in the B movie playing on the huge Imax screen. The fire roared engulfing the entire room, all the bad actors were in a panic.

Suddenly as the movie continued to play, the screen looked as if it were ripping, tearing, melting away. In fact, it was. A portion of the screen was burning away by flames it seemed to blend in with the flames from the movie almost camouflaged. The fire was behind the massive screen, the movie continued to play with this hole burning away in the center. Panic swept the room, similar to that when the ship exploded earlier. People were screaming out in fear, they began scattering in different directions, trampling over each other and the Black Coats. One of the Black Coats tried to stop them by firing off a few rounds killing a few people, but he was quickly over taken by the crowd and trampled to death himself.

I held Mary tightly to my chest, she whined in panic. There seemed to be nowhere to run. The flames were soon everywhere, smoke quickly filled the room. I looked from the left and to the right for an escape route but to no avail all the hostages had quickly flooded the three main exits to the point they were densely packed in like a can of tuna. Screams of horror filled the large theater like an opera house when the fat lady sings. Maybe it's over just as the old saying goes 'It isn't over till the fat lady sings,' but I wouldn't give up that easily. Not Kenneth Gill, son of the infamous Robert Gill, the second who single-handedly saved the lives of sixteen people in burning building downtown in 1947. I still remember the papers headlines. -**LOCAL HERO ROBERT GILL SAVES LIVES WITHOUT THINKING ABOUT HIS OWN.**- That was the headline of the Chicago Tribune, the very next day dated August 4th 1947. That day though is nothing in comparison to today, August 12th 2005. I can see the headlines now -**LOCAL HERO AND SON TO FORMER LOCAL HERO SAVES LIFE**

LIVES YET AGAIN NEARLY 60 YEARS LATER.- But that's enough delusions of grandeur for now.

"Grandpa I'm scared."

"I know Hun, I am too." I eased my way through the narrow seating still holding onto Mary and trying my hardest not to loose my balance. The smoke was growing thicker as we moved forward in the direction of the fire. I thought for a moment that this was not the ideal way to go if we were to get out of this, but there was no other way. We had to get through the mob of people flooding the exits. We stood a better chance of survival going straight into the flames then risking being trampled by the mob.

"We're almost out of..."

"Stop right there!" A Black Coat yelled aiming a gun straight at my head.

"Please the building is a blaze! Just give us a chance! I beg you!" The gun shook in the young Black Coats hand. He seemed nervous as if he would be punished if he let us go.

"I'm warning you."

"What will you get by killing an old man and a little girl?"

"Don't move." His lips quivered as his eyes moved rapidly.

"A medal? Perhaps a pat on the back. Well done. You managed to kill two innocent people knowing full well the entire place was about to go up in flames."

"You just shut your face!" He exclaimed with a hint of uncertainty. I thought for a moment that perhaps I had somehow got through to this man. Even in the most minute amount.

"Come now, Sir. You should be trying to save yourself. At any moment this whole place will be engulfed and then at that moment it will be too late. Is that what you want?" This time there was no reply. He lowered his eyes to his feet almost ashamed of his behavior and then he lowered his gun.

"Thank you." I simply said as I was about to move past him. Suddenly I was stopped by a huge flaming timber that came crashing down at breakneck speed killing the Black Coat in an instant. I shook my head and averted Mary's eyes.

We continued on through a narrow corridor. I had know idea where this would lead us or if we were just heading to a dead end. Mary seemed numbed by the whole thing. I tried my hardest to comfort her, but I could feel my own confidence slowly fading. Not to sound cliché, but there was a light at the end of the tunnel. I ran to it, and on the other side we were in the main shopping center. The fire did not seem to have got this far but the smell of smoke definitely lingered in the air. There was a large map posted on a lit up billboard in the center of the walkway. One of those -**YOU ARE HERE**- signs. I franticly searched for the exit. I found the little arrow pointing to -**YOU ARE HERE**-, and found the path leading out. I ran in the direction passing a storage room where I heard a crash from inside. I paused for a moment, and shook my head continuing on.

*   *   *   *

Doc and Jerome

*   *   *   *

"Aw, man! I keep tripping over this damn mop…excuse my language." I said to the kid but it didn't seem to phase him either way. I had no idea how much time had passed since that lady cop dumped this kid on me, but he was not much of a conversationalist. This little room was getting to me and I needed a fucking cigarette. All I could do was wander aimlessly through it tripping over mop buckets. The small light bulb that lingered over head rocking back and forth as if it were mocking me, was the focal point of my restlessness. I sighed in frustration rubbing my face with both hands. I sat down on a flipped over bucket resting my arms limply on my lap. I looked over to the kid, and wondered about his name.

"So your names Doc, huh?"

"Yes."

"How'd you get a name like that? What from Snow White and the Seven Dwarves or something?" He shook his head.

"What then?"

"My Daddy gave it to me before he died." Maybe I shouldn't ask anymore questions, don't want to get on a touchy subject by mistake with this kid. Still my curiosity about the name, and the fact that I was bored as hell consumed me.

"So what does it mean?"

"One time my sister was drowning in our pond in the backyard, and I pulled her out, and I saw this thing on TV about uh…what's it called again? CPR? Yeah, that was it, so I used CPR to save my sister. Ever since then my daddy called me Doc." I looked at him amazed.

"How old are you kid?"

"Five and a half."

"Wow." My jaw practically dropped. A five year old kid who knew CPR and saved his sister's life.

"That's amazing Doc, I am impressed." Doc looked at the watch on his wrist shaking it a little causing it to move loosely on his arm. I rested my head back on the wall mumbling to myself about needing a cigarette.

"You shouldn't smoke." I blinked rapidly being disturbed from my rambling under my breath.

"Excuse me?"

"You shouldn't smoke…I was watching Health Watch on the ten O'clock news, and they said smoking causes lung cancer and…what's the word? Oh emphysema, which leads to heart failure. And new studies have shown that light and ultra light cigarettes do not better your chance of not having health problems." I shook my head in amazement.

"Man, I'm sitting in a room with Doogie Howser."

"You know what else I learned on Health Watch? That woman in there thirties with other health problems are more prone to get breast cancer…"

"Alright, alright. That's enough." I rubbed between my eyes with my index and thumb. "Shouldn't you be into Blues Clues, or Dora the Explorer or something?"

"There mentality of education is to primitive for me." I closed my eyes thinking I was better off not starting a conversation with this kid, he might just be smarter then me. That's when I noticed the sudden change in atmosphere. It was starting to smell like smoke. I rose to my feet peaking out the door to the hall. The whole area was filled with black smoke.

"Shit kid. We got to get out of here!" I took Doc's hand in mine crouching down low beneath the smoke. I covered my mouth with my shirt and instructed him to do the same. We made our way through the halls, my eyes were watered and sore. I coughed and choked on the smoke and then somewhere up ahead, I could make out what looked like a man in a firemen's outfit come running this way. I thought for a moment that this was the end. The cavalry had finally arrived. It was over. That's when I fainted.

*   *   *   *

Still 8:37 PM

*   *   *   *

"Fuck! This is not good." I said to Mira.

"Not good is an understatement, John." The screen was ripping apart piece by flaming piece. The burning pieces of the screen floated down onto chairs starting them on fire. Some would land on hostages burning them. Most of the hostages packed the exits so tightly they were practically stuck, jammed in like a herd of cattle. The fire was spreading quickly, all I could think of was any possible way to control the situation, but my thought's were interrupted when out of the sky a hatchet came flying at me, barley missing striking the wall behind me. I knew right way it was my nemesis from before. I looked up to the catwalk, he stood there atop it gripping the rails smiling down with his evil scarred face...Axe

"Mira, find Wes Adams. I have some unfinished business to take care of."

I climbed the stairs slowly and unarmed, except for the knife I drew, it would be the weapon of choice. My eyes never left the attention of that one milk white glass eye. He stood there at the top of the stairs looking down upon me, arms folded knife in hand. I thought about drawing my gun and ending this swiftly, but I had no idea how fast my nemesis was on the draw, I knew he was quick with the hatchet, therefore he must be equally quick with the gun. I had no desire to take that chance, so now I will face him hand to hand, blade to blade, once more in what I hope will be my final battle with this hideous abomination called Axe. In all the years I have fought criminals in combat such as this, I have never faced an enemy so difficult to kill. I had stabbed him in the side. He lived somehow without any medical attention none so ever. Judging by his many scars though, I knew I was not the first to try and kill this man. I believe he loved it, a sort of immortality.

"Mindless drone." He said with an evil low pitched snicker. I was not yet at the top, still about ten steps away looking up at him. I slowed down even more, not looking forward to the fight ahead.

"You gave me this." He opened his coat pointing to the huge open gash in his side. "In exchange for that." He referred to the wound I had wrapped with a torn fabric around my leg.

"It is a symbol of a great warrior, you should be proud to bare the mark of the Axe. Only few have been able to bare the mark of the Axe and live. Tell me mindless drone, have you figured out why you are here?" I was up to the last two steps looking him deep in the one good eye he had. Replying softly to him.

"Here let me kill you first and then I'll buy you a beer and tell you." I said.

He stepped back leaning forward knife held blade down in one hand and the other behind him in a sprint stance. I mimicked him lunging forward, he jumped back. He lunged I jumped back. We fought one attempting to strike the other but always blocking. We were making our way little by little to the back of the theater where the catwalk was at it's highest point.

"You are a worthy adversary drone, though you are a mindless one." I said nothing in reply continuing to fight with the knives. They clanged making a sharpening noise every time they touched.

It was an intense fight for sure. Two men of equal strengths and skills, a continues stale mate as it were. Finally something let up, but not to my favor I might add. He had me up against the rail pushing me back with his forearm to my neck, while he held the knife high ready to strike, I struggled to keep him at bay.

"This is ludicrous drone. We are equals, good vs. evil, arch enemy's in a comic book tale. Neither of us shall die or it would be the end of the story." I huffed struggling.

"No offence, but I hardly know you and I would like this story to end sometime today." He grinned that disgusting grin.

"This is true drone, we have just met earlier this day, but I have known about you for a time now." I was puzzled, he did in fact know my name, and I never spoke of it to him.

"How do you know me?" I managed to push him back and snuck in a stab to his other side. He winced and tried to strike me, but to no avail I dodged his attack.

"Fool, never trust those closest to you. A slithering snake can sneak in undetected and return a message to its master." What was he implying, that he sent a snake under my office door? He grabbed me by the neck and put his face close to mine whispering.

"You became very acquainted with my pet snake." Ignoring him I stabbed him in the stomach, he turned pale with a blank stare. I thought I had killed him, I was wrong. He stepped back looking down at the knife in his stomach, blood protruding down his dark clothes. He breathed in deeply as he pulled the knife from his body crying out in pain. He looked at the knife with a smile, it dripped with his blood. With an act of admiration he handed my knife back to me. I took the knife and the battle continued. I slashed his chest, he merely laughed. I stabbed him in the shoulder, again he laughed. It was a game to him like children at play. I tried to stab him in the heart, but he grabbed my arm before I had the chance, looking me in the eye with that sinister face. I winced in pain. He lightly stabbed me just below my chest. Only a few inches, then he moved it in a few more, and a few more.

"To die a slow agonizing death, is not what I would wish to happen to myself, but to you I see no harm in it." I knew if the knife goes any deeper it would all be over. I remembered my trusty Jackknife in my back pants pocket. With my free hand I reached in and grabbed it. I said to him grinding my teeth.

"This fall will be nothing in comparison to the fall you'll experience afterwards." I took the tiny little Jackknife and drove it into the center of his forehead, a little trickle of blood ran down to his nose, he looked at the blood cross eyed. With great force I pushed him over the edge. This would be a wound that will never scar.

*   *   *   *

Weak and losing blood, I made a generic bandage out of what's left of my shirt, and wrapped it as tightly as I could. I griped my torso as I limped to the room that Wes must be in. I went to turn the handle but it was locked.

"Open up, Wes." I exclaimed.

"John? Is that you?" He replied in a low voice.

"I know you were behind all this Wes, game over." there was a short pause and then he replied.

"You know I cant do that John, and besides I have a hostage in here, Mr. Johnson." I sat down on the floor resting against the door. I was to weak to stand.

"I'll blow this fucking door handle right off if you don't open." I rolled my eyes back closing them.

"Then I'll kill Mr. Johnson." Where was Mira,? I thought?

"Wes you were a good friend of mine, and served well on the force. I can get you off easy, maybe even less then ten years." I sat there practically falling in and out of consciousness, This was not the time to pass out I thought.

"Wes, there's a fucking fire out here, you have to come out." I looked down the hall. It would only be a matter of time before it made its way down here and we would be stuck inside burned alive.

"I can't go to prison, John. Do you know what they do to cops in prison? I can't be locked up and fed to the scum's I put away. I won't!"

The clock was ticking, It was only a matter of time now before a thousand S.W.A.T.S, F.B.I, Cops, even the military came through here. "Why did you do it, Wes? How did you get mixed up in all this?" I could tell by the sound of his voice he was close to the door maybe leaning against it.

"Have you ever been asked to do something you knew was wrong but you had to make the choice or the consequences would destroy you? My family John…" He paused.

"I like every one else, the Mayor, the Commissioner, and Mr. Johnson here, knew about the Black Coats. We were going to expose them…but something happened." He paused for a moment.

"What?"

"They got to me."

$$* \qquad * \qquad * \qquad *$$

It was about six months ago, I had just spent the entire day with the Mayor and the Commissioner discussing the possible existence of the Black Coats. It was far too clear that they did in fact exist. All the evidence was there. All we had to do was think of way to gather the attention of the masses in subtle approach. I had gone home late that night with thoughts about our approach. My children were already fast asleep. I woke Sally when I entered the bedroom.

"Wes? Wes is that you?" I started to unbutton my shirt in the dark.

"Yes." She moaned a little and fell half back to sleep. I crawled in next to her with my dress pants still on. I was too tired to take them off. I laid there placing my hands under my head, looking up at the dark ceiling. Just thinking about The Black Coats. Eventually I fell asleep.

I was woken up by the feeling of someone pressing their hand with a leather glove to my mouth. I opened my eyes only to see a hideously deformed man leering down on me. He pressed one finger to his lip in hush gesture. There were five or six of them in the room alone, all armed with semi-automatic weapons. They were taking my wife into the next room along with my two children. It was Axe. He was sent by them to take care of me.

"Wes Adams?"

"Who are you?" He pulled out a shiny steal meat cleaver with a bronze handle.

"They call me, The Axe."

"Your one of them aren't you?" He looked at me with milk white eyes.

"One of whom, may I ask?"

"The Black Coats." He smiled and did not answer. Instead he stood up and walked around the room.

"Lovely home you have here, Wes. The family portraits all over are a nice touch." He paused.

"Do you love your family, Wes?"

"Don't you dare harm them." He spun around.

"Presuming already, are we? Who says I'm going to hurt them?" He sat back down at the edge of the bed holding the meat cleaver in his hand.

"It's funny, Wes. If you kill someone with a gun you're a murderer, but if you kill someone with a gun and then proceed to chop them up into small pieces with a meat cleaver you're a psycho." He paused and looked at me.

"Are you a psycho or a murderer?"

"Neither."

"Is that so? What about Eric Brownstone?"

Eric Brownstone? How did he know? Eric Brownstone was a civilian caught in the crossfire. There was a violent standoff at a fast food restaurant on the lower eastside. I infiltrated the building and by my own mistake shot the first person I saw holding a gun. It turned out he was a vigilante that happened to be at the wrong place at the wrong time, with the wrong cop busting through the door. The actual perpetrator had already fled and was never found. There was a cover up and Eric Brownstone took the heat to save my own ass. The actual perpetrator is still out there somewhere.

"That was a mistake."

"Maybe it was, but you still could have admitted to your wrong doing and the real man would not be running around free right now."

"What do you want?"

"You to disavow any existence of the Black Coats or your career is over."

"I refuse you can tell them anything you want, but you will be exposed."

"Oh, anything? Even about your little affair?"

"What?"

"You know damn well what I mean. Tilly Titillating down at the Titty bar." He said with a grin.

"How did you? I never meant for it to go that far."

"It doesn't matter now. What's done is done. And unless you cooperate I will go into the next room and tell your wife and kids what Daddy has been up to in his spare time."

I was at a loss I had no choice. I could never live with myself if they knew. I had to agree to do as Axe said.

The very next day I told the Mayor and the Commissioner that I would have to respectfully decline from engaging the Black Coats. That was the last time I spoke with them. A few months later I received another visit from my heavily scarred friend Axe. It struck me as odd because this time he came alone and walked right up to the front door, ringing the bell. I had been sitting there watching television with my family. I looked out the window to see him standing there with his hat held in hands in a polite manner. I told Sally to take the kids upstairs and wait until I came to get them. I answered the door.

"I have job for you." He said smoothly.

"Come with me."

I followed him to a black sedan with tinted windows. They drugged me and I spent the next three months training for this day. I haven't seen my family since.

*   *   *   *

He stopped there. I reached in my pocket for my Tylenol, I downed five or six pills. "I didn't want this to happen, John. It was supposed to be a clean sweep. We were to blow up the ship, killing the Mayor, and inadvertently a few nearby innocents. Then Block was to pick us up shortly thereafter. He was the one who was going to take the fall for the Black Coats. He knew it, but he excepted it. He called it sweet revenge for what the Mayor did to him. Things just got way out of control and away from the plan and Block never showed. He'll have to suffer the consequences the Black Coats will bring on him for that mistake. They'll likely have him eliminated soon enough. John, The Black Coats are not amateurs. Aside from today, they have never had a single mistake in one hundred years." My heart dropped, and my face went pale.

"How long did you just say?" He replied with no change in his tone of voice.

"One hundred years. They have been responsible for a countless amount of conspiracies in the U.S. for the last century. There are more of us out there who know of there existence. We are on the dawn of a new civil war in America. Today was just the beginning John and now you are involved, they will come for you John. I'm sorry to say but your time is also near end."

I stopped and thought about all Wes was saying. It was the most unbelievable story I had ever heard. "What about the government? Why don't they know?" I looked down at my wound. The blood had stopped.

"Who's to say they haven't known all along? There funding them John. If a job needs to be done and the government does not want to take the blame, they hire them to do the work." Terror consumed me. If all Wes was saying was true, then the future looked very bleak.

"Who's the leak?"

"What leak?"

"Who told them what the Mayor and the Commissioner were up to?

"I'm sorry I can't answer that, John. I really don't know."

The fire was growing closer, we had to get out. "Wes, it's over now, you'll be safe in prison. They won't come for you there." I could tell he was pacing around now.

"No John, I'm too far gone already. They won't tolerate the mistakes I made today, they will tell my family everything, and even if they don't, I could never rot in prison I would sooner die…There is only one option left."

There was a long pause, then I could hear Mr. Johnson cry out. "No Wes, don't!" A gun shot and thud came next. I rose up to my feet and shot the door handle off kicking it open, with my gun ready I ran in. Mr. Johnson was alive and tied up in a chair. Wes lay dead on the ground. A bullet to the head from his own gun he still held in hand. I lowered my head and ran my hand down my face, it was over.

"We have to get out of here, Mr. Johnson." I quickly untied him, his hands and ankles were purple from chafing. We started to make our way out the building when a huge flaming timber fell from the ceiling, blocking our path.

"Fuck!" I cried out as I looked around. "Do you know any other ways out?" Mr. Johnson thought for a moment.

"I believe the wall in the storage room maybe weak enough to break through. They seem to be working another part of the island on the other side, it's just simple dry wall." I remembered the construction site where the Commissioner's men dropped down on us. There was a small section covered in plastic that looked like it was simple drywall.

"Lets go!"

Inside the storage room I raced to the back wall. I moved a filing cabinet off to the side and kicked the dry wall in. My foot went through making a small hole, I kicked it again and again. Finally, I made a hole big enough for both Mr. Johnson and I. There was plastic, I was right. I tore through the plastic.

We were back at the construction site. It was now dark outside the night air was cool and refreshing, the lake water made for a nice breeze. The sky was completely clear of any clouds. The stars shimmered in the night sky. You could see the city sky line, it was the most beautiful thing to lay eyes on. All the buildings lit up in a variety of different patterns, creating the perfect portrait. I could not wait to get back to that portrait, and off this God forsaken Island. I stood there for a moment with Mr. Johnson we were both beaten, tattered and bleeding. We gazed out to the sky line.

"Its beautiful isn't it?" Mr. Johnson nodded in reply.

"The most beautiful thing I have seen all day."

We made our way around to the other side of the island, where all the commotion was. All the hostages were scattered throughout the island, some embraced their loved ones as if they had not seen them in forever, even though they to were hostages today. They held each other like they had not seen each other all day. It did not matter, they were happy to be free again. Others talked away on there cell phones to friends and relatives, telling them they were okay, it was all over now…at least for them it was.

Choppers of every sort filled the sky above. There were police, S.W.A.T., military, and paramedics everywhere, many of which had already landed. They were scattered all over the island, escorting people off the island in handfuls. Paramedics were everywhere. Mr. Johnson and I passed two that were actually helping a woman going into labor.

"Push, Mrs. Feldman, push."

"Oh, I can't it hurts, I don't want to have my baby here."

"It's gonna be alright, Mrs. Feldman." She cried out as she sat on the uncomfortable looking stone bench.

"Look at that, Officer Paddock." Mr. Johnson said as we walked by.

"As it has been said before, with death comes new life, humanity carries on and continues."

I thought about what he said, and the War that Wes said would come. "Lets hope we don't destroy ourselves before life is given a chance."

Some of the bodies from the ship explosion still lay scattered about the island. Some stacked in piles being prepared to be taken off the island to a morgue. While others lay gruesomely in there original stance. Severed heads and missing limbs scattered about in washed away pools of blood. It was a dismal and depressing sight in the mix of relief, but what depressed and disgusted me more was the fact that our government may have had something to do with this. It made me want to vomit. I fought the urge. The thought made me more sick then the actual sight. Red and blue lights flashed everywhere, the island was still a blaze, the flames made for yellow a reflection on everything mixed with the blue and red. Police boats pulled up and docked the island. Men in body armor, and heavily armed, ran around in all directions inspecting the area, searching for anymore possible Black Coats. I could tell them they were all dead, but would they listen? I doubt it. I, along with my team, single handedly took them out and saved the day. Speaking of which, Mira was still nowhere to be found.

*   *   *   *

9:05 PM
Going Home

*   *   *   *

Mary and I sat on a park bench as the paramedics raced around gathering up all the most needy ones. "Grandpa? When do we get to go home?" How do I explain this to a child?

"Well, Mary do you remember when you broke your arm playing at the park?" She nodded.

"And then your mother and I took you to the hospital, but there was a boy there who had been in a car accident. Remember we had to wait for the doctor to finish with him first because he needed more attention then you or he could die." She nodded again.

"Well, its like that honey, there are people on the island who need to get to the hospital before we do. So we will just have to wait." She put her head on my shoulder.

"Okay Grandpa, but can we get ice cream later?" I hugged her with one arm and smiled.

"Of course, Mary."

*   *   *   *

Doc

*   *   *   *

"Officer Paddock!" It was Doc, the little boy I had rescued earlier. He was being carried by a fire man. His clothes were charred with black spots, and his face was covered in soot. Jerome was following close behind, also covered in soot.

"Doc! How you doing buddy?" He smiled.

"Great! Mr. Jerome saved us from the fire and then the fire man came and saved us two!" I smiled at him, he still had his fathers watch around his wrist.

"Guess what, Officer Paddock." I looked at him and shrugged.

"What?" He looked around to the skyline pointing towards it.

"I'm going to go home and see my mommy." I rubbed his dirty soot covered hair.

"Great Doc, I bet she misses you." He nodded.

"Yeah. Okay see you later." I waved him goodbye. Jerome stopped and smiled.

"Hey thanks for taking care of him Jerome." I extended my hand out waiting for his response.

"Hey no problem officer, the little guy kept me company in there. Did you know how smart this kid is?"

"No."

"He's smart. Very smart. Kids gonna be a doctor some day."

He looked at my hand that was still waiting for his handshake and finally shook it.

"You take care now." I said. He looked around.

"You do the same, say where's your girl at?" I rubbed my chin.

"I don't really know. I was just going to go look for her." He started to walk away and said with a side long glance.

"You better find her man, she's a good woman." I thought about it and replied under my breath inaudible as he walked away.

"I hope so."

The Chopper that the Commissioner had rode in before made another appearance out of the night sky. Ironically, it landed on a patch of flowers, the last bit of beauty left on this damned island. Once I saw the cloud of smoke released from the chopper I knew it was him.

"Excuse me. Mr. Johnson. There's someone I have to go speak with."

The cloud of smoke around his face had already been regenerated by the time I reached the chopper. Only his lower body and a few random patches of his face were visible. I didn't care though, I would be able to find that face in there. I walked right up to him he extended his hand to shake. I extended mine as well, only to punch. I hit him in the face right through that cloud of smoke. He stumbled a little. A nearby officer looked at us with concern. The Commissioner with that cloud of smoke around his face looked over. He told the officer it was alright.

"You fucking son of a Goddamn mother fucking bitch!" I yelled. He took a puff from his cigar.

"You set me up! You knew about this all along and you set me up!" He shrugged raising his arms still holding the cigar.

"John, I did tell you. I told you every day subliminally, so you would dream about it every night. A small microchip about the size of a pinhead was planted inside your cerebral cortex. All of you, Chuck, Bobby, and Jack. It's purpose is to alter your dream patterns in such a way that you would be training for this in your sleep. The idea was we could tell you everything you needed to know without actually telling you. No questions, no concerns. It was an astonishing way to fight the war. Your susceptibility to the program was quite satisfying."

That would explain all the crazy dreams I have had for the last two years but he forgot to mention one thing.

"You didn't mention, Mira. Why was she not implanted?" I asked the question, fearing the answer.

"We did, sort of. She was implanted the same as the rest of you, but there was a problem with the program, a glitch, a bug if you will. It was as if someone scrambled it. It was too costly to go ahead with the procedure again. So we had no alternative but to terminate the program, and the Mira files, and simply work on you, and the others.

"Why? Why me? Why? I don't understand. Why did you pick me?" He took in another puff.

"Because John, you were the most qualified for the job and you did well. I knew you could handle it." I looked around at all the death and destruction. I threw my hands up in the air. "Tell me, what have I done? Seriously the Mayor is dead, a countless amount of innocent civilians are dead, almost my whole fucking team is dead asshole! And your going to tell me I did some great thing today! What!?"

He started to walk around me slowly. "You have proven you're a true General ready for the war to come. Yes there have been casualties. It's a given with any war. And now that the Mayor is dead, it's only a matter of time before the Black Coats are exposed. I knew the same as the Mayor, that this day would come. He knew the sacrifice that he was going to have to make for freedom. He knew to expose the Black Coats would probably cost him his life. As I told you before, we are all expendable. Congratulations John, you passed the final test."

I stood there hand on my hip still in great pain, but not ready to see the paramedics yet. "So that's it. I was trained to fight in this grand war you keep talking about. A war against a bunch a mother fuckers I have never even heard about up until today. I'm just another one of your puppets, is that it? Well I don't want your fucking war! I could give two shits and a fuck about you or your goddamn war or any of your other bull shit! I quit! I'm done!"

I started walking away, as my back was turned he continued to talk. "You will be back John Paddock, once they come for you and believe me they will. You'll have no choice. You will be back." I did not turn around as I flipped him the bird with the back of my hand.

CHAPTER 15

▼

Denial

I walked the island passing and ignoring all the commotion around me. People being checked out by paramedics, police running around scanning the area, all the people who would stop me and say officer, can you tell me what's going on. I cared not for what they had to ask, only depression and confusion consumed me. I did not even know what was going on. It was this torment that drove me mad and made me wonder what I was really here for. I was lost in thought, wandering the island aimlessly, thinking to myself, my life for the past few years had been nothing but a lie, an endless sea of betrayal. I could trust no one now. I could hardly trust myself. It was like a bad dream. That whole thing about mind control scared me. There is a chip right now in my head. Who knows what else they could do with it. Maybe they can read my thought's right now. Who was I even anymore? Was I John Paddock or did he die like the rest of my team? I wished I had. I wished I could trade places with Chuck or Jackie, or even Bobby for that matter. At least they died knowing or at least believing they were fighting for a greater cause. At least they died with honor, with pride. Honor and pride were two things I had lost.

I have tried to live a good life. I have tried to help people, to do what's right. I know I can be a womanizing, belligerent, arrogant ass who thinks I know it all at times. But I generally consider myself a good man, at least I did. Maybe I deserve this? Maybe this is my punishment? Who were the Black Coats anyway? Why should I give a shit about them? I think I would be better off never knowing they even existed.

What will I do now? Move up north maybe, find a new job in construction or something. Start a new life, a life without the Black Coats, or the Commissioner and all his bullshit. Yeah, that sounds good. I wish Mira could be in that life with me.

* * * *

The Tour de Michigan

* * * *

The tour de Michigan? What in hell is this? I asked myself. A huge white civilian yacht was docked at the island on the other side, out of sight of ground zero. It's name read The tour de Michigan. Why was this yacht here? Michigan? Block was supposedly living in Michigan. I decided to check it out.

Inside the lower half of the yacht was a large dining area all the chairs were turned up side down atop the tables, no one was around. It was dark, only a few lights were turned on. Slowly I crept my way through the dining hall, there was a stairway leading up to the upper half. I drew my gun as I slowly made way up, ready for anything after a day like this. I could make out the faint sound of voices coming from above.

The top was a living room with expensive looking leather couches, glass tables and oak finish walls, it was extravagant and rich, the kind of yacht that seemed unlikely to be owned by someone like Block. There was a large Plasma screen TV, and an ash tray with a single cigarette butt still burning in it. I made my way slowly to the slightly cracked open door, light was shining out of it, I placed my head to the door to listen to the conversation.

"Mira what happened to the rest of the Black Coats?"

"I don't know Block, when I left John Paddock was fighting Axe, and Wes was still in the room with Johnson…and what the fuck took you so long to get here anyway, Block?" Mira? She was the leak? I thought to myself.

"I had a few problems that needed to be dealt with in Michigan. It's really none of your concern."

"Whatever, my guess is that John Paddock killed Axe and Wes Adams…there it's done over, we should get going before they notice us."

"You have much faith in this John Paddock, do you not?"

"Well he is good, for a cop."

"Good for a cop? Interesting statement. I think maybe the reason he is so good is because you did not do as you were instructed, you were supposed to eliminate him remember?"

"Well…I had no choice, he interfered with the plans too much." Block chuckled a little.

"Is that so? Tell me again how you had all those conversations with Jackie just before you met up with John."

"I already explained this to you, it was about an hour before the incident with the Commissioner."

✳   ✳   ✳   ✳

She went on to explain about the events that took place before I met up with her and Jackie in the mall with Doc in my arms. She sounded nervous and unsure of herself. I couldn't believe what I was hearing. The woman I trusted and loved betrayed me. Rightfully so, everyone else and their mother has this day. It seemed to be a superhighway of betrayal. I must have been Adolph Hitler in another life to deserve all this. Mr. Block interrupted her.

"I see, so that's how it is. You were just so busy helping him that you completely forgot…oh my god that's right I'm supposed to kill you, how silly of me…I don't buy a fucking word of it. It sounds more like you got to attached to him, I'm thinking yes? All those other Black Coats here today, died because of you bitch." I heard a slap and thud.

"And now you have placed my own life in jeopardy."

"It was not my fault Block and anyway you should have been here hours ago to pick us up off this Godforsaken island. So if any one is at fault it's you." There was a long pause. I sat there in anticipation waiting, wondering what happens next, or if I should even get involved. Pondering the fact that helping the woman who betrayed me was not in my best interest at the moment. The sound of a gun cock was all I heard.

"No bitch, I wont take the fall for you! I'm going to tell the Black coats this was all your doing." It was now or never, I had to do something. My brain told me walk away. She betrayed you. It's not your fight anymore, I said to myself. But my heart told me how much I cared for her, she had her chance to kill me and she didn't. Maybe this would be the greatest mistake of my life, but love is a idiotic emotion that plagues us all.

"Drop the fucking gun now!" I busted into the room kicking the door open with my chrome desert eagle 45 in hand. Mira was on her knees, Block had his gun point blank, aimed for her head, she bled from her eye from Block's strike. A look of puzzlement came over Block's face as he turned to look at me. Two members of the Cheng Sun clan dressed in red and black dragon robes were standing on my sides armed with AK's the two bald Chinese men with there brows narrowed did not look friendly. Block was a middle aged, balding man with glasses. He was overweight and the ridicules red and yellow dragon robe that was similar to that of the ones the two bald Chinese men wore except instead of black it was yellow, did not help his weight problem, he was not even Asian for that matter. I'm not exactly sure what ethnicity he is, but I'm sure it's not Asian. The room was similar to the last, except this one had a bar lined with liquor bottles, expensive ones at that, featuring a half empty bottle of Belvedere vodka, about a shot left of Cabo Wabo tequila, and a rare bottle of Johnnie Walker Blue label. Two leather love seats across from each other which is where Mira and Block stood between. This was a Mexican stand off, without the Mexicans, every man armed, aimed, and cocked. Anyone could pull that trigger, and whoever dies is anybody's guess.

"You must be the great John Paddock I have heard so much about." He said to me keeping his gun steady on Mira as he looked at me.

"And you must be the great asshole I'm about to blow away if you don't drop that fucking gun." He exchanged glances with the two Cheng Sun Clan members.

"I don't think my men here are going to let you do that." I looked at them with side long glances, there expressions hadn't changed.

"Besides, why should you care what happens to her, she's one of us, she was supposed to kill you." I looked at Mira, she never looked more ashamed in her entire life. Her lips quivered as she was on the verge of tears.

"Yeah well, she didn't, right now I don't know why but…" She interrupted with a shaky voice.

"Because, I love you." It was the three little words I longed to hear, but never did I imagine I would hear them like this. A smirk started to take over my face, I got a little cocky with that.

"Yeah, what now? You here that, bitch boy. She fucking loves me. Yeah, what?" Maybe a little to cocky. Block rolled his eyes.

"I'm deeply touched, this is truly a moment they should make a Hallmark card for. It would say something along the lines of, oh dearest husband, I could not kill you because I love you." I looked at Mira she was trying to smile.

"Kill him." Block said. I instantly dropped to the floor to dodge the bullets, they pulled their triggers simultaneously killing each other instead. I laid on the ground aiming my gun at Block's head. I had the momentum, the upper hand. All I had to do was pull the trigger, but that's not how it went. Suddenly a chopper hovered outside, shinning its lights through the window, almost blinding me from seeing anything in front of me. Without warning a mini gun attached to the chopper started to fire, shattering all the windows. Block fell dead on the leather loveseat arms hanging over the sides, his red and yellow dragon robe now laced with to many bullet holes to count. Mira fell to the ground. I cried out as she fell. It could not be possible, not after all this.

The chopper took off, leaving me there to deal with the pain. I wished it would have taken me as well. I crawled over to her, she lay there looking at me still breathing. "I wont let you leave me, not after I finally have you." I took her hand in mine she looked so cold.

"John, please listen to me. What I wanted to ask you before." She coughed and continued.

"I want you to take care of my daughter, she loves you, and your great with her..." I shook my head holding back the tears never wanting to let her go.

"Everything's going to be fine." I said as she ran her hand down my cheek.

"I have to go John, it's the only way. You'll understand later I promise...I have made a lot of mistakes, but meeting you and falling in love was not one of them." I could not hold back the tears any longer my heart was ripping apart.

"Please take good care of her..." She used her last bit of strength to kiss me. It was a kiss I would never forget, one I had long waited for. She closed her eyes, and was gone. I laid there next to her and passed out from blood loss.

*   *   *   *

10:45 PM
Truth is a Transparent Lie

*   *   *   *

I open my eyes the lights of cameras flash, the sound of muttered voices all around. A detective hovered over me looking down upon me.

"You awake?" He asks. I sat up, looked around, I was still on the yacht.

"Where's Mira?" The detective pointed to the side of me, she was on a gurney bed about to be hauled away, her head faced me, she looked so peaceful. Something startling and surreal happened, it took my breath away. It was as if she opened her eyes for a split second and shut them quickly. A haunting image to see.

"Wait, did you see that? She's alive, she's alive." The detective shook his head at the paramedics. They took her away.

"No son, I'm afraid she's not. You're a little delirious right now, you have lost a lot of blood." I shook my head.

"No it was them…they killed her." The detective frowned with a look of puzzlement.

"Who? Who killed her?" He asked. I tried to stand up but was weak from blood loss, the detective helped me to my feet, there were homicide detectives, and forensic cops taking pictures, and samples all around. It was a crime scene within a crime scene.

"The Black Coats. Wes said they would come for Block, and they did, but they killed Mira in the cross fire. It's the Black Coats. I'm telling you the fucking truth." The detective gave a nod like he did not believe me but went along with it.

"Alright, alright, why don't you just sit down, son. We're going to get you to a hospital soon." I shook my head stumbling like a drunkard. "Goddamn it! Why don't you believe me?" A paramedic pulled out a syringe, sticking it into my right arm. I was out like a light.

✳   ✳   ✳   ✳

8:45 AM
Lutheran General Hospital, Trauma Unit

✳   ✳   ✳   ✳

The hospital was filled to the brim with patients, most of which were from the island. I was actually in the hall because all the rooms were full. There were all sorts of different problems with each patient. One man was a burn victim covered head to foot in third degree burns beyond recognition. Just across from me was a young child, who's mother stood by his side, gripping his hand in hers, he was out cold, and had been so since the first explosion. She prayed for his life.

Nurses and doctors ran around like chickens with there heads cut off, doctors from all over Cook County were called in off duty, every doctor in the city was paged. Emergency operations were made right next to me in the middle of the hall. I imagined a war zone and these were all fallen G.I. The doctors were military medics in the middle of a battle field. Bombs and grenades dropping all around, machinegun fire raining down from the sky. Every now and then I would find myself having flashbacks of the war. In fact, I had them so often I would find myself day dreaming all the time.

"Thank you for your time, Officer Paddock." I said standing there beside him. John Paddock lay in the gurney draped in bed sheets. His side and leg bandaged from knife wounds. Diastolic and systolic wires coming out of his chest and forehead. A blank look on his face, as if it all were just a dream, and perhaps maybe it were.

"No, thank you, Doctor Gibson. I'm glad I was able to tell someone my story." I patted his hand with a smile.

"And your story will be told to all. These Black Coats must be exposed, once the general public hears of their existence we will be able to stop them." I paused for a moment. "Oh yes, I have also been collecting other stories from a few other people. One Mr. Johnson says hello." He smiled with a nod.

"Mr. Johnson? I only met him towards the end." I brushed of my gray trench coat sleeve.

"Yes, that's what he said as well." I looked at a clock on the wall. "8:45 already? I guess I better be on my way. My wife is expecting me with breakfast waiting on the table. It's been a long night, you know." I held my note pad and tucked it away in my briefcase. John Paddock looked at me and nodded slow.

"Yes it has. Yes it has. Thanks again doctor, I have confidence that the truth will be exposed and this so called war will not have to happen." I smiled and tipped my gray fedora, bidding him farewell.

✳   ✳   ✳   ✳

Behind the Dark Curtain

✳   ✳   ✳   ✳

I wiped my glasses clean as I walked down the hall along side of Officer Specter, an older, medium build man with a receding hair line. He had a smug look as he asked me a question.

"What do you think, Doc? Is he out of his mind?" I breathed into my glasses wiping them more.

"Without a doubt. He's suffering from delusions of grandeur, posttraumatic, shell shock. He's finding a way to pin the blame on someone else for the loss of his team members." The officer nodded in reply.

"Yeah, pretty sad. To bad too, he was a good cop." He said to me almost with no remorse for John Paddock. I questioned whether or not he truly cared. Perhaps now with John Paddock out of the way, officer Specter was up for promotion. I placed the glasses back on.

"I will schedule outpatient visits after his discharge. Unfortunately, in this case I don't think he will be returning to the force anytime soon…if at all." He sighed transparently, seemingly in an effort to hide his lack of concern.

"Thank you for your time, doctor." I gave him a slight consoling grin, not that I think he cared, and then was on my way.

I continued to walk down the hall, I was a psychiatrist hired to analyze people and their problems, or so they thought anyway. As I walked that hall no one paid attention to my presence, just as they never have before. The nurses ran around the same as the doctors, never giving me a second glance. I was another shadow just passing through. As I walked that long hall towards the main entrance, I thought about all the stories I was told today about the Black Coats. What would the future hold now?

My shiny black loafers tapped upon the tile as I walked, all the muffled sounds of voices were blocked from my mind. The weeping sorrow of an old woman was hardly audible to me. Nothing of my surroundings was of any concern. The doorway grew ever nearer, it was all that stood between me and destiny. I passed a guard sitting on a chair his arms folded over his popped belly. He simply glanced up to me as I passed and nothing more, not a second glance was made.

Outside was a beautiful day, one not nearly as hot as the previous night, more a cool 80 degrees. The sun was hidden behind a single cloud and the rest of the sky clear as water. I stopped and stood there on the steps, proudly taking in a deep breath of fresh air, then continued my decent. The area was crowded beyond belief. People were everywhere, whether or not they were coming and going or simply standing still, it did not matter. No one paid attention to me and why should they? I was just another face in the crowd, nothing more then a shadow.

As I made way through the crowd, I placed my briefcase on the ground and removed my gray trench coat turning it inside out. It was now a black trench coat. I put it back on and removed my gray hat, with a quick punch to the middle it went from gray to black. I placed it back on my head, leaned down, and opened the briefcase. There was nothing more then the simple note pad and pen inside. I looked at the note pad. It was full of nothing more then smiley faces that I had doodled while listening to Officer Paddock's boring story. I smiled and closed the briefcase. I rose to my feet removing my thick bottle glasses and replacing them with a pair of dark shades.

Yes, I would now journey into the dense crowd, never being noticed or given a second look. It was the same as it always was, the same as it always will be. We will continue to walk the night, the shadows, the dark alleys, never seen or heard. We will remain…behind the dark curtain.

To Be
Continued

978-0-595-35819-9
0-595-35819-5

Printed in the United States
35059LVS00012B/61-63

9 780595 358199